SKYLA GRAY

The Nightmare's Kiss

Monster Research Facility #1

Contents

Chapter One

Stepping off the plane and back into Ash Valley doesn't feel like coming home. It feels like retreating with my tail between my legs. Or—since I'm feeling especially dramatic today—maybe more like limping home from a lost war with nothing but the scars to show for it. Except in this case, the war is college and the scars are a useless degree and a whole lot of student debt.

It's humiliating, returning to the tiny town I swore I'd never return to. I worked so hard to get out of here. When I first received my acceptance letter from USC, I cried from happiness. I was even a little smug about it, to be honest; no one had expected much from little Mara with the wild hair and skinned knees.

Now, here I am. Back to the dust and the heat of small-town Arizona.

Coming from LAX, the Ash Valley airport is stiflingly quiet and empty. Half of the restaurant options are shuttered even though it's midday, leaving a single, sad coffee stand and a booth selling some incredible looking nachos. But even that only makes me think of all the Los Angeles food I'm going to miss.

The fact that one of my suitcase's wheels is sticking feels like being kicked while I'm already down. I grumble as I yank it along, already starting to sweat even though I haven't stepped out of the airport and into the sweltering glare of the sun yet. I eventually give up and lift the bag in my arms, waddling ungracefully until I reach the escalator.

It eases the sting when I look down and see my parents waiting for me near the luggage pick-up area. I haven't seen them in person in almost a year. I had convinced myself that video calls were enough, but the pang in my chest right now is an argument to the contrary. God, I missed them.

My dad is stoic beneath his mustache, as usual, but he's craning his neck to look for me in a way he probably thinks is subtle. And my mom, standing next to him, looks ecstatic. When she sees me, she jumps and waves her hands like I might not notice her in the almost-empty airport.

I manage a small smile, and cradle my bag awkwardly with one arm so I can wave. There's a very short list of things I love about my hometown, but my parents are on it.

And they look good. I worried that my leaving would be hard for them, but it seems like they've adapted well to the empty nest. As I reach the end of the escalator, I notice that they both have new lines on their faces and streaks of gray in their hair, but they look happier, too.

"Sweetie," my mom says, throwing her arms around my neck and hugging me around the bulk of my suitcase. "Oh, honey, welcome home."

It doesn't feel like home. *Home,* for the last few years, has been a tiny studio apartment with walls full of horror movie posters and a neighbor who plays soft jazz every evening. Friday nights with my friends and cheap wine. Quiet Sundays spent lounging in bed, enjoying my solitude. But I don't tell her that.

"I missed you," I say, because it's kinder and still true. Once she releases me, I set down my suitcase, step over to my dad, and hug him as well. He pats me on the back, clearing his throat; it feels lackluster, but I know he's just not very good with emotional moments. My mom, meanwhile, is sniffling quietly at his side. "You both look great."

"I've been getting your dad to join me on my morning walks," my mom says, dabbing at her eyes. "And yoga, occasionally."

I raise my eyebrows at him as I pull back from the hug. I'm trying to imagine him doing yoga, with his mustache and his stern expression, but I just can't wrap my head around it.

"Lies and slander," he says, stone-faced.

"Maybe you can join us next time," my mom says, perking up.

My lips curve into a smile. Early morning walks and yoga do not sound like a good time to me, but it'd be worth it to witness my dad participating. "As long as he's there."

My mom continues chattering as I go to retrieve my luggage, giving me updates on her garden and the neighbors and the changes to the school board. I nod like I'm listening while a quiet devastation grows in my chest. God, this is what I've definitely *not* missed about living in a small town: the sleepiness that gives people nothing better to do than gossip. Everybody sticking their noses into each other's business. My return will likely be the talk of the town in a place like this, and I'm not eager to face the judging eyes and probing questions.

The moment we step outside, the heat hits me like a physical weight. Away, it was easy to forget quite how this feels—like the very air is oppressive, so hot and dry it seems to suck the moisture out of me with every breath. My feet drag, every step taking extra energy, the heat of the asphalt radiating through the soles of my sneakers. I imagine I can feel my skin sizzling on the short walk to the car.

My dad insists on grabbing everything other than my carry-on suitcase himself, despite my protests. He huffs and puffs his way through the parking lot, his face beet red and increasingly sweaty as we make our way out. But I can barely handle my suitcase with its faulty wheel, so I can't offer much assistance, and he'd rather die than "make" me or my mom carry anything anyway. My mother, oblivious, trails behind us and continues talking.

"Oh, and Ethan Mayhew is back in town," she says, a sentence that cuts through the blur of other noise.

I jerk to a stop, and then pretend it was just to adjust my sweaty grip on my carry-on. "Oh? I didn't know that."

"Don't you keep up with him on the internet?" she asks, blinking blithely.

"I don't go on social media much," I lie. "It's for old people now, Mom." The truth is that I have him blocked on all platforms, but she doesn't need to know that. Nobody needs to know the truth about what happened between me and Ethan—especially since I doubt they'd believe me over Mr. Oh-so-Perfect.

"Oh, well," she says, flapping a hand. "Anyway. He moved back… a year or two ago, I think? Not sure what he's doing here, a smart boy like that, but rumor has it that he's working at the *Facility*."

She speaks the moniker in hushed tones, as people tend to do. And that bit of news catches my interest more than the stinging comment about *a smart boy like him*, as if I'm not stuck in this small town too. "I didn't know they hired locals."

"Me neither. But then again, there aren't many locals with a college degree, huh?"

"Hmm." I turn and look off into the distance, though the Facility she named is currently hidden beyond the buildings of the town proper. "Interesting." *Very* interesting. I resent my own curiosity, but I can't fight it. The Facility is the best—and only—mystery this town has, and I've never had such a personal connection to it before.

"I thought so, too. So I suggested to his mother that you two should have coffee sometime, talk about your options around here. Maybe Ash Valley isn't the dead end you think it is."

She beams at me, clearly pleased with herself for the idea, and I force a half-smile. I can't say no to her when she's looking at me like that, so I mumble a vague assent, even though I have no plans to see Ethan, if I can help it.

Thankfully, we reach the car and conversation dwindles as my dad and I heave my luggage into the trunk of his beat-up old Civic. I slide into the backseat while they take the front. It's hot enough to make me wince—and I remember just in time not to touch the searing metal of my seatbelt after it's been sitting in the sun. *A nice Arizonan welcome*, I think, as I carefully finagle it without burning myself.

After a few minutes of driving, I lean my forehead against the window and tune out the sound of my parents' cheerful bickering about what to make for dinner. I watch familiar roads and buildings rush past, sprawling expanses of desert full of prickly cacti and not much else, and am struck by a mingled feeling of nostalgia and despair. Everything about Ash Valley looks exactly as I remember it, like a snapshot of my memories. But I have changed too much to feel like I belong in this picture, if I ever did at all.

* * *

My childhood home, like the rest of the town, looks exactly the same as it's always been. My dad boasts about the repairs to the fence and the fresh coat of white on the door, and I make some agreeable noises, but honestly the whole thing looks the same way I remember it. But once I step inside, a strange feeling washes over me. Everything looks familiar, cozy in a southwestern cottage kind of way. My mom has a taste for color and desert hues, all dusty rose and ochre with pops of turquoise, along with some frankly dizzying geometric patterns.

Yet the house seems smaller than I remember. Like the ceiling is too low, the doorways too small, the walls slowly closing in on me. It gives me a weird sense of vertigo, like I'm dreaming and just realized everything is a little bit wrong, but I shake it off as I remove my shoes and head inward. The floorboards all creak in the same places, a pattern I memorized as a teenager with a tendency to sneak out.

My dad makes us a delicious dinner of chicken and dumplings, and I'm delighted to discover that he now wears an apron my mother bought him last Christmas reading *King of the Kitchen* while cooking. He lets me take a picture of him wearing it, spatula in hand and lips pressed into an unamused line, but only after I swear up and down that it will not end up on any of my social media pages. Dinner is nice, and comforting after the stress of the last few months. Still, I'm already craving the privacy and space I became used to while I was away. I'm grateful when my parents start yawning almost immediately after eating and bid me goodnight.

I step out onto the back porch to take a few guilty but soothing hits off my vape. As I blow out mouthfuls of pineapple-flavored vapor, I look out over the sleepy town. Ash Valley couldn't be more different than LA. It's not even ten p.m., but already most of the lights are out. People and businesses shut their doors, calling an early night in anticipation of an early morning.

Except for one building on the outskirts of town. A boxy silhouette glowing in the darkness.

There have always been rumors about the Facility. People agree it popped up on the outskirts of Ash Valley sometime in the fifties, and most assumed it was a government outfit relevant to the Cold War effort. That's about all people can manage to agree on, though. Everyone has a different idea about what's really going on behind those electrified fences and windowless concrete walls. Some think it's a secret military prison or a testing site for new weapons. Others say MK-Ultra, or a psy-op training facility, or another government program.

Each potential explanation is more ludicrous than the last. If you ask me, the place is probably far less interesting than rumors would suggest. It's certainly something classified, given the fact that it's still standing decades after the Cold War's end and security has only grown tighter, but I'd bet it's nothing more interesting than physical copies of old government documents, or nuclear waste, or something like that.

Either way, the Facility is a constant presence. Ash Valley is a small town, and it's the biggest building around, a conspicuous gray block amid the dusty plains and cattle farms. But growing up here, it became easy to forget about the Facility eventually.

It was just a fact of life, an ever-present background image, like the mountain peaks that mark the horizon. Some nights there would be rumors of strange noises from the building, or helicopters circling overhead, or lines of armored trucks rolling through the gate, and the rumors would kick up again. But the excitement always died down, life went on, and people forgot.

But now, it's like a beacon in the otherwise dark town. I can't take my eyes off it. I take a few more comforting puffs of vapor and then dig my phone out of my pocket.

"Mara!" My friend Amy answers on the third ring, as expected.

I grin at the sound of her voice, though there's also a bittersweet tug in my chest. "Hi, hi. How's it going?"

"Good, busy. How about you? How's the small-town life?"

"Ugh, you know." I grimace, not too eager to get into the details. She makes some sympathetic noises and doesn't pry, which I love her for. "Even *better* with the news I got upon landing… Apparently, my ex is back in town too."

"*The* ex?" she asks, well aware of my history with Ethan after some late-night, drunken heart-to-hearts. There have been other boyfriends and girlfriends over the years, but none of them cut me as deeply as Ethan did.

I take another nervous puff of my vape. "Yup. My mom is pushing for me to meet up with him."

"I'm guessing she doesn't know the details."

I sigh, sinking into a rocking chair. It's surprisingly comfortable. "It's not easy to talk about."

"No, yeah, I totally get it."

I chew my lip, staring out at the city. At the Facility, specifically. I can't stop thinking about my mom's mention of him working there. I wonder what he's doing behind those walls. "Is it crazy that I'm thinking about it? Meeting up with him?"

"For what? Closure?"

I hesitate. *Is* there a part of me that wants that, or needs it? Not really. I feel like I got more closure from therapy than I'd ever get from meeting with him. I'm much more interested in learning about the Facility, but I can't really explain that to her. A mysterious high-security building in the middle of the desert, and not even people who grew up here know exactly what goes on there—it'll sound nuts to anyone who hasn't lived in Ash Valley. It's easier to tell a little white lie. "Yeah, I don't know, maybe?"

"I mean, I wouldn't. But it's up to you and what you think you can handle, babes."

"Yeah…" I sigh out the word and sink further into the chair. "But, anyway, enough about my shitty life. Tell me about LA!"

As I had hoped, it doesn't take more than that to get Amy chattering. She provides a welcome distraction from the ache of being so far away from her. I relax as I listen to her, making encouraging noises when appropriate and dragging out some lurid details of a recent sushi dinner. *God, am I gonna miss good sushi.*

Yet even as I try my best to follow my imagination to the bright lights and great food of Los Angeles, my eyes keep drifting, again and again, to the silhouette of the Facility.

And after I hang up, against my better judgment, I click on a phone contact I haven't thought about texting in a very long time and shoot off a message:

I hear our mothers are conspiring to arrange coffee between us. Should we indulge them before they go through the effort of an elaborate setup?

There's a little anxious twist in my stomach as I send it off. Still, when I get inside, I fall asleep the second my head hits the pillow.

Chapter Two

Waking up in my childhood bedroom is a surreal experience. As I stare up at the textured white paint of the ceiling, dotted with a few glow-in-the-dark stars that somehow never fell off, I feel a strange sense of déjà vu, like I'm reliving a day from years ago. My parents left my room untouched. The walls are still plastered with embarrassing posters of boy bands and Sailor Moon. Above the headboard dangle fairy lights and strung-together Polaroids of friends I haven't spoken to in years.

Outside my door, the rest of the house is quiet. It's a Monday, after all, and both of my parents must be at work already—my dad at the local home improvement store, and my mom at the library. I spend a good, lazy half hour in bed on my phone. But my email inbox is empty, scrolling through the news is depressing, and my social media pages even more so. Everywhere I look are pictures of my college friends moving into exciting new apartments in exciting new places for exciting new jobs. Meanwhile, I'm here, stagnating in an old twin bed that's even more uncomfortable than I remember. I've told my parents it's just a tough market right now, but the truth is that I've hardly applied to anything. Every time I look at the requirements for a job or a master's degree, it makes me feel like I want to puke. The endless requirements, the low pay, the fact that I'm one of hundreds of psychology students who graduated from my university alone... How the hell am I supposed to stand out? What makes me special?

The answer I always settle on is: nothing. Nothing at all. And so I exit the page before I can bring myself to submit my resume or transcript, every time.

Before I can wallow too long in my despair, a text lights up my phone. *Free for lunch today if that works?*

I rub my still-bleary eyes and sigh. Coffee with an ex who's more successful than me sounds like the last thing I need on my first day back in town. But I'm the one who offered, and I know that if I don't use this excuse to drag myself out of bed, I'll probably spend the rest of the day wallowing. Plus, my mom did mention—several times, pointedly—that my dad would drive them both to work so she could leave her car here for me to use as I wish.

Anyway, in a town this small, it's inevitable I'll run into Ethan eventually. Better to get it over with now, in a situation under my control that I can adequately prepare for. Otherwise, it'd probably end up being on a midnight alcohol run in my pajamas and day-old makeup and be even more embarrassing.

I sit up with a groan, shoot off a thumbs-up text, and drag myself out of bed to prepare.

* * *

The moment I walk into the cafe and see Ethan waiting at a table in the back, I'm grateful for the time I spent getting ready. I felt foolish applying make-up and pulling on one of my favorite outfits—a wide-leg floral jumpsuit and cute Chelsea boots—for an ex I don't even *want* to see again. But now, seeing him in a button-up shirt and sporting an admittedly flattering new beard, I'm glad I don't look like I just dragged myself out of bed…even if it's true. I still feel half asleep without my morning cup of coffee, but my parents only have one of those nasty fake-coffee pod machines in the house, and I wasn't desperate enough to stoop to fake coffee when we had plans at my favorite cafe.

Cup o' Happy does not disappoint. I breathe in the rich, earthy smell of freshly-ground beans, listen to the frothing of the espresso machine and the low chatter of conversations at the tables in the back, and a sense of calm washes over me. I spent so many weekend afternoons here as a teenager, sipping sweet mocha out of handmade mugs or downing shots of electrically bitter espresso. While some things have remained the same—there's still the usual chalkboard of specials on the wall behind the bar, and a collection of kitschy mugs to choose from if you're not taking your drink to go—there are also fresh touches that make it feel less stuck in time than the rest of this town. Someone has added playful doodles along the specials list, which also includes several drinks I've never had before, and the windows have been updated to allow more buttery sunlight to spill across the pastel flooring.

I'm also relieved, in this case, to see that some things are the same. Eloise is still standing behind the checkered counter, and resident café cat Schadenfreude curled up atop the register. Eloise's hair has gone completely white, and there are new lines in her brown face, and Schadenfreude looks even mangier than I remember with his matted gray fur and half-missing ear, but they're still here.

Eloise's face lights up as she sees me approaching. "Oh, darling, you're *back*," she says, leaning over to take one of my hands. Her hands are dry and papery in the way of the elderly, but her grip is still strong around my fingers, and her eyes are still bright. She's dressed in her usual bohemian style, in a flowing chiffon dress with chunky, colorful jewelry heaped around her thin neck. She's seemed vaguely old since I first met her as a young teen and seems older still now, but she still radiates the same exuberance as always. "I've missed you, dear."

I smile, squeezing her hands. "Missed you too. And your coffee. *Desperately.*"

She scoffs as she pulls her hands back. "Oh, pishposh. I'm sure they had decent coffee somewhere in that big ol' city."

"Not like yours," I say, and I mean it. I eye the selection of mugs and then grab one with a frowning sunflower and present it to her. "Surprise me with one of the new specials?"

She beams. "Oh, yes. I've got something I think you'll love." Then her expression shifts, and she leans over, lowering her voice to a whisper. "By the way, I should warn you, a certain ex of yours is lurking in the back corner."

I suppress a laugh. "I'm here to meet him, actually, but I appreciate the heads-up."

She lifts her eyebrows but doesn't ask any questions. "Just tug your earlobe if you'd like me to pass by and spill hot coffee on him," she says, and busies herself preparing my drink.

I lean over to scratch Schadenfreude atop his head. He opens one eye to glower at me for disturbing his rest and then shuts it again. I'm pretty sure he's secretly pleased.

With that done, and Eloise promising to have my drink

delivered to the table once it's ready, I have no further reason to delay. I turn, set my shoulders, and walk to Ethan's table.

He's typing on his phone, and only looks up when I stop beside the empty seat across from him. But as he raises his eyes to meet mine, a smile spreads across his face, and he shuts off his phone and stands to greet me.

"Mara," he says. "Been a while." Before I can try to guess what the proper greeting is, he extends a hand to shake. It feels oddly formal, but less weird than a hug probably would be, so I lean over to accept. He pulls out my chair for me, too, which is a nice touch, and not at all something I would've expected from the version of him I used to know.

"Thanks," I say, taking a seat. He sits across from me and sips his espresso.

"How long have you been back in town?" he asks.

"Just got in yesterday."

"And how long are you planning to stay?"

"Uh…" I wince and shrug. "Good question. Ask the job market, I guess?"

"Ha. Right. You majored in…what was it?"

I suppress another wince, this one of shame. "Psychology."

"Oh." It's a knowing *oh*. An "oh, damn, that's not gonna get you a job anytime soon" kind of *oh*. "So, do you intend to go into therapy, or research, or…?"

"I'd need more school for either of those, and I'm not so sure that academia is for me," I say—the tried-and-true, practiced-in-front-of-a-mirror answer.

I see his mind working, coming up with the obvious next question: *So what's your plan?* Thankfully, he chooses to discard it. "Well, it's a broad field. I'm sure you'll figure out some way to apply it."

Gratitude flushes through me. It's a kinder response than I expected from Ethan, but I have to remember, this is what he does. He's always nice, until he isn't. "Thanks," I say. "Speaking of applying yourself… I heard a little rumor about what you're doing back in town."

He chuckles, leaning back in his seat. "This town does love to gossip."

"Especially about…you know," I say, waggling my eyebrows.

"Right." He cups a hand around his mouth. *"The Facility."* His mocking, hushed tone is an uncanny imitation of the way my mom said it last night, and I can't help but laugh. But beneath the amusement, I'm also relieved. If he's able to joke about it, the place can't be as nefarious as people make it seem. Right?

"So it's true?"

"It is. Though I'm really not allowed to talk about anything that goes on in there, so please don't ask."

"Not even a hint?" I ask—mostly teasing—but he only shakes his head.

I manage to pry a few sparse details out of him, such as him working there for going on two years, meaning he was hired straight out of college, but after that he goes tight-lipped again.

"Come on, Mara." He leans forward slightly, still smiling. "I know you didn't ask me here just to ask about the Facility."

"Uh…" Oops. I've been caught.

"The truth is that you want to ask for details about my life without admitting you want to know. Am I right?"

The hint of a smirk suggests he believes he's right on the money, which is *much* worse than him catching me out in my scheme. But openly dry-heaving at the thought will definitely burn this potential info source, so I force a smile and scramble to find a middle ground. "Well, to be honest, it's also the fact that you're one of the few other college grads in town, and I'm looking for job leads."

I expect his ego to be mollified by that, but instead he lets out an incredulous huff. "Oh, well, you're definitely not going to find that at the Facility."

It hadn't even occurred to me as a possibility, but his immediate dismissal of the thought irritates me. "Why is that so ridiculous?" He got hired just out of college, didn't he? "Is the work highly specialized?"

"No, it's—" He pauses, realizing he almost gave away information, and gives me a thin smile. "It's a very high-stress work environment, let's put it that way."

Great. Now I'm annoyed he thinks I can't handle it *and* annoyingly curious about what he's trying so hard not to tell me.

I'm spared the struggle to find a civil answer as a shadow spills across our table. I look up, expecting to see Eloise's summery form, but instead startle as I find an unfamiliar stranger looming over me. A teenage stranger wearing black, including lipstick and eyeshadow, with a streak of neon green dyed in the dark curls that frame her brown face.

"Your latte," she says stiffly, placing my frowning sunflower mug in front of me. Its expression matches hers almost comically.

"Oh, tha—"

"I was also instructed to ask if you need me to spill a hot beverage on your conversation partner," she says in a flat tone, her eyes fixed somewhere above my head.

I blink. Blink again. "No, thank you," I say, and she shuffles off without another word. I turn to Ethan, baffled.

He smothers a laugh into a cough behind one hand. "I see

you haven't met Blaire yet?"

"Most definitely not," I say.

"She's Eloise's niece. Visiting for the summer. And she's… well." He shrugs. "You saw."

"Yeah," I agree, glancing after her. She's walking around delivering other drinks around the cafe, her presence like a dark cloud hovering over whichever table she visits. "Customer service does not seem to be her forte."

"You can say that again."

I take a sip of my drink and hum in pleasure, closing my eyes to savor the flavor. It's deep and complex—sweet but not too sweet, with an underlying savory note that almost reminds me of… "Butter?" I say, opening my eyes.

"Ah, the maple brown butter latte," Ethan says, with a nod at the specials board. "Bit rich for me, but I've heard it's very popular. One of Eloise's newest creations."

I sigh, cupping my hands around the mug and taking another slow, meditative sip. This is the perfect remedy to the lingering bitterness of Ethan's words to me. "She is a creative genius. A queen of coffee."

Ethan grins. "I see your love of caffeine has not changed," he says, leaning back in his chair and slinging an arm across the back. "You seem different, though. Better. More grounded."

Ah. There it is. One of those comments that comes out in such a mild tone, like he's being nice, when we both know that what he's really implying is that there was something wrong with who I was before. *Grounded* is code for *more mature*, as though I should've or *could've* been "mature" when I was a teenager. Or maybe it's code for *less crazy*, since that was another one of his favorites to throw at me. The sting is emphasized by his earlier implication that I can't handle a "high-stress work environment."

Once, it would've made me feel small. Now, I'm surprised by the ferocity of the anger that rises up within me. I clench my hand around my coffee mug, briefly entertain the thought of tossing the hot drink into his face, and force myself to take a sip instead. Breathe in, breathe out. I hate feeling so impotent, but if I show anger, he'll only turn it against me. "How are your parents?" I ask once I lower my cup, and thankfully, he accepts the change in topic.

The conversation flows more easily than I thought it would from there, but each time I try to circle back around to the Facility and his work, he nudges me away so gently, I hardly realize I'm being redirected. It isn't until he's walking out the door and I'm staring at the bottom of my empty mug that I realize I didn't get a single bit of information about the Facility...other than the fact that it's too "high stress" for me.

And, of course, that makes me more determined than ever to find out the truth.

Chapter Three

I return to Cup o' Happy the next day to start my research into the Facility anew. I'm much too proud to reach out to Ethan again, but that doesn't mean I'm ready to stop snooping, especially after the way he tried to brush me off over it. Where does he get off on implying he can handle a "high-stress" environment better than I could? Now I *have* to find out what's going on there, if only to prove to myself that he's not doing anything nearly as important as he implied. It can't be as cool and interesting as people think it is; it simply can't be, if they were willing to hire someone like Ethan straight out of college. I have to debunk the theories. Plus, I have way too much time on my hands, and the Facility is the only interesting thing about this town.

And, if I'm being honest, I *desperately* need something to cling to right now to stop myself from falling into a well of despair. Refreshing my empty email inbox all day is going to make me sick, and I physically cannot bring myself to apply to more underpaid jobs.

But I want to do *something*—to learn, to apply myself somehow—and this seems like a perfectly decent coping mechanism. The thought of spiting my ex is just a delicious little cherry on top.

So I order a lavender latte and decide to start my impromptu investigation by interviewing Eloise. She's a lifelong local, and it seems like as good a place to begin as any.

"So, random question," I say, leaning over the counter to watch her make my drink. "Do you know anything about the Facility?"

Her hands go still, hovering near the machine, before resuming their work.

"Nobody knows anything about that place, honey," she says, her voice carefully neutral.

"Sure, that's what everyone *says*, but it can't be true," I argue. "It's been here for so long, so close. And you've lived in Ash Valley all your life, right?"

"Mmhmm," she murmurs, her gaze focused on the coffee machine.

"You never learned anything about it?"

"Never did, never wanted to," she says. "Place gives me the heebie-jeebies."

"But if you had to *guess* what they're doing in there—"

"I'd rather not," she says, handing me my mug with a brittle smile. "Now move along please, honey. I love ya, but I've got work to do."

The cafe is almost empty on a Tuesday afternoon, but I take the hint. Yet when I turn to make myself scarce, I find myself face-to-face with Blaire, wearing the same intense black makeup as last time I saw her. "Oh, uh, hi?"

"You're asking about the Facility," she says. There's a gleam in her normally flat eyes that takes me by surprise. "I have some thoughts."

"Really?" I glance over my shoulder at Eloise, who is

pointedly ignoring us, and then usher Blaire over to a table in the corner. Instead of sitting, she looms menacingly over me while I sip my coffee. "So you know something?"

"Well, I've read all sorts of things on the forums," she says. "It's part of the reason I wanted to come here for the summer. I wanted to see it for myself. Of course, I haven't gotten any closer than the fence. Yet. Did you know about the string of disappearances when the Facility first appeared here in the 1950s? Or the second time in the 80s?"

I lean forward, captivated despite the fact she sounds like a conspiracy theorist. "What disappearances?"

She looks me in the eye and whispers, "Exactly."

I pause for a second, expecting her to go on, but apparently that's all she's got. I lean back in my chair and repress a sigh of disappointment. For a second there, I thought I was going to hear some real evidence. "Okay," I say slowly. I already regret engaging with this, but she's still looking at me expectantly, and I feel obligated to hear her out. "So assuming there were disappearances, how do you know they're linked to the Facility?"

"Officially? They're not." She folds her arms over her chest. "But who else would be powerful enough to sweep all of that under the rug?"

It's not exactly compelling evidence. Still, right now, I'm just grateful to have someone willing to talk to about this. "So what's the internet's theory, then? What are they doing there?"

"There are a couple different schools of thought," she says. "But if you ask me? The most likely one is that they've got a portal to *Hell* in there. And every thirty years they need to make sacrifices to keep the devil from escaping."

I finish my coffee quickly and get out of there.

* * *

I drop by a few other local businesses, visiting old acquaintances and buying treats I've missed in the city. Along the way, I pepper in questions about the Facility whenever I can. But over and over again, I face the same responses. There are the people who refuse to talk about it, like Eloise, and the people who are too eager to discuss their outlandish ideas about it, like Blaire. Each new conspiracy theory is more ridiculous than the last. The Facility is really housing a secret military prison, or a luxury bomb shelter for the rich and famous, or an experimental government program developing superhuman soldiers.

A man in sweat-stained overalls at the deli tells me he occasionally catches snippets of coded messages on a radio station late at night. A nervous woman at the local donut shop insists we both turn our cell phones off before informing me in hushed whispers that she was once abducted by aliens, and swears the Facility had something to do with it.

The more nonanswers I receive, the more curious I become. The Facility has been here for decades. How is it possible that nobody has concrete information about it? Nobody even knows what the place is actually called or who owns it. Aside from Ethan, nobody local works there or knows anyone who does. His name comes up several times, often with a curious side-eye as they realize I'm his ex-girlfriend, but nobody knows what he does there or why he was hired when no other locals were.

By the time I get home, I've sweated through my T-shirt from the heat of the day, as the poor old AC in my mom's car struggles to combat heat over 100 degrees, and I'm no closer to an answer. This is probably the point where a normal person would give up. But I am a bored, unemployed, understimulated, stubborn person, and my spite is renewed with every admiring mention of Ethan being the only local to work there, so I dig deeper.

I check local news outlets for coverage. Nothing. I travel to the library—and say a quick hello to my mom behind the counter—to search their records. Nothing. I scour the internet. *Nothing.* That's even stranger than the rest. The Facility is missing from Google Earth and Maps, and there's nothing about it on the website for Ash Valley or anywhere else I search. As though its very existence has been carefully wiped away.

The only place I find any traces of it online are some ten-year-old local message boards where the users are all anonymous. The original user posed the question: *Anyone been hearing strange noises at night in Ash Valley?* The conversation that follows starts off normal—people suggesting that it might be a mountain lion that wandered too close to town, or a pack of coyotes, or some bored local kids causing a disturbance. But then someone mentions a couple of local disappearances, and someone else brings up the Facility, and the conversation quite quickly derails into conspiracy theories and urban legends.

Not too far out of the ordinary for the internet. The stranger part is that the last three pages of the conversation are all deleted messages. When I click on the usernames, I see that none of them have posted on the forum since this conversation happened. Frowning, I scroll back up, and stop at one of the last messages before all of the deletions.

"THEY ARE HIDING SOMETHING."

I stare at it, tapping my fingers on my mouse.

I don't want to believe Ethan's hints at his own importance... but I'm starting to feel like whatever is happening in that building, it's quite a lot bigger than our humble little town.

* * *

At dinner, I tell my parents about my findings—or lack thereof—over a delicious dinner of steak and potatoes. I expect them to laugh either at or with me, but instead they both seem nervous when I tell them some of the ridiculous theories I've heard.

"I think you should be careful who you talk to about this, sweetie," my mom says, giving me a pained smile. "There are a lot of weirdos in this town with strong opinions about that place. You don't want to attract the wrong kind of attention."

I give her an incredulous look and then direct another at my dad, who is conspicuously silent at her side. He grumbles quietly, looking down at his meal instead of at me.

"I don't know what's going on in that place, and I don't want to know," he declares.

The theories may be different, but it seems that everyone here feels the same: some mysteries are better left unsolved. Even my normally grounded parents are no exception. It should probably encourage me to give up. But stubborn bitch that I am, it only makes me want to do the opposite.

* * *

The next day, I wake to a knock on the door. I drag myself out of bed and shuffle out in my pajamas and slippers, ready to inform whichever neighbor or delivery person is here that my parents are out for the afternoon. But when I open the door, I'm faced with a stranger.

That's odd enough, in a town this small. But even odder is her style.

Her sharp heels, crisp trousers, and silky blouse have no place among the farms and mom-and-pop stores that make up most of Ash Valley. Her clear-framed glasses and elegant dark bob look too modern for the place too. She comes off wealthy and educated, and something about the casual way she drapes her blazer over one shoulder feels intimidating—especially because *nobody* wears a blazer in Ash Valley, especially in the summer. When her eyes meet mine, the hair on the back of my neck stands up, and I feel a chill despite the already-warm morning air.

The fact I don't recognize her, plus the too-professional clothes, can only mean one thing in this town: she's from the Facility.

"Hello, Samara," she says, as though we're old friends rather than total strangers. "I think it's time we had a chat."

Chapter Four

I shouldn't let her inside. I know I shouldn't. Everything about her and the fact she's on my doorstep screams *danger*. But I've been hunting for answers, and I have a sneaking suspicion that she might be able to provide some. So, despite my better judgment—and my embarrassing Hello Kitty pajamas—I soon find myself ushering her out of the heat and into my parents' house and offering coffee. Once it's ready, I meet her in the dining room with two cups, feeling as though I'm walking into a spider's web.

As I set her cup in front of her, my eyes rake over her in a search for any hints about the nature of this visit. Am I in trouble? In danger, even? But I find nothing in her expression or demeanor. She's middle-aged and frankly gorgeous, with perfectly manicured fingernails and a watch that looks expensive. She smells faintly of tobacco smoke and floral perfume.

I slide into the seat across from her, sip my coffee—bleurgh, fake pod machine coffee—and say, dumbly, "Hi. We don't know each other, do we?"

Her smile is sharp. "No," she says. "But you seem so very curious about my workplace, which made me very curious about *you*."

My throat tightens. I suspected this, but still, the confirmation gives me goose bumps. I thought she would at least come up with a less creepy way to say "we know everything people do and say in this town," but this was pretty blatant, and now I'm wondering if all of those conspiracy theorists had the right idea. "You're from the Facility."

"Yes. Dr. Calliope Wright."

"Samara Vance," I say automatically, though she already called me by name.

She folds one leg over the other and rests her hands in her lap. "You've been asking a lot of questions, Samara Vance."

I flush, bite the inside of my cheek, and fight the urge to be defensive. I haven't done anything wrong, even though this feels like I'm a problematic child called into the principal's office. "Everybody has questions about the Facility." Even though she named herself, I note, she did not give any indication of what to call the building itself.

"I expect that's true, but you'd be surprised by how few actually *ask* them. Most, I suspect, do not actually want to know the answers. They prefer to speculate, or perhaps they're afraid of what the truth may be." She leans forward. Her eyes are an intense green, and I can't look away. "But you're not afraid."

I swallow. "Should I be?" I intend for it to be a joke, but it comes out more like a challenge.

She regards me in silence. Then she leans back in her chair and smiles like she's learned something that satisfies her. "You earned a degree in psychology at USC, is that correct?"

"Yes," I say, and swallow an instinctive *ma'am* that wants to tag along.

"There aren't a lot of job prospects for such a degree in Ash Valley."

I nod. What else is there to say?

"And that's a shame," she continues, "because you seem like a very promising young woman. Great marks, no trouble on your record, experience in a professional lab setting. You were a tech for a research study about sleep disorders, correct?"

"Yes, that's—"

"Your former supervisor spoke highly of you," she continues without waiting for me to answer. "Strong work ethic, good under pressure."

I startle. "You talked to…?"

"But what really caught my eye was the essay you wrote in Abnormal Psychology," she says. Her eyes go a bit distant, wandering above my head. "'Even delusions maintain their own internal logic, and if we hope to understand the patient, we must indulge their version of the world, no matter how far it may be from our own. For who are we to claim that our reality is the only one?'"

I hardly remember what I wrote in that essay, but I know she just quoted it from memory. I suppress a shiver, unsure what to say. "What is this about?" I ask—whisper, really.

Her eyes snap back to me.

"Despite local sentiment, the truth is that the Facility is eager to foster relationships with those who live in Ash Valley," she says. "However, it must also be said that there are few among the population with the proper education or background for the type of positions we are looking for. You, however, are a unique case. We believe this could be a valuable opportunity for the both of us. And as such, we would like to offer you a job opportunity."

It takes me a couple of seconds to digest that. I stare at her across the table. "A job," I repeat. "At the Facility."

It feels like a bad joke, but her expression is serious. "It is an entry-level position, but there is plenty of opportunity for advancement if you are able to perform your role well."

"Okay… And what would I be doing, exactly?" Despite my bewilderment at this whole situation, I find myself leaning forward slightly, eager to finally get some of the answers I've been seeking. "What kind of work do you *do* at the Facility?" I ask, before realizing she's already dropped some hints. Lab work. Research. "What are you studying?"

Dr. Wright offers a sliver of a smile, but rather than giving a response, she clicks open her briefcase, takes out a thick stack of papers, and slides them across the table to me. My eyes scan the first page, heart thumping as I wonder if this is a chance to sate my curiosity, but I find only further exasperation.

"An NDA," I say, unable to hide my disappointment.

"Indeed," she says. "And I am afraid we need you to sign it before we reveal more information about the nature of our research or the position we are offering. Especially as…" She hesitates for a moment. "Well, it is easier to show you the work you will be doing, rather than explain it. We need your agreement before we can allow you within the Facility. But rest assured, we will not consider this an acceptance of the offer until you have all of the information you require."

An NDA isn't a surprise, especially when the Facility is obviously secretive, but having the agreement in front of me suddenly makes this feel a lot more real. My heart rate spikes as I read further. Not only am I forbidden from writing about my work in any public forum, or taking any pictures or videos, or even bringing a cell phone or any other "digital device" into the building. I'm also not allowed to take personal notes out of the building, or speak about it to anyone, *ever*, for the rest of my life.

What could they possibly be doing within those concrete walls? As I scan through the pages, I only become more certain that I'm walking into something stranger than I expected. It has to be something military, or government related, just like the rumors suggested. Something important, as Ethan hinted at, even though I really didn't want that to be true. Possibly something that will challenge my morals.

Then I reach the final page, which includes a brief outline of the job they're offering, including the pay. I go still, my finger resting just under the listed figure like I'm trying to reassure myself it's really there. My eyebrows shoot up as my mouth forms an expression that must be comical. I glance up at Dr. Wright's impassive face, and then back down at the number, and it's still the same. *Generous* would be putting it lightly, especially for entry-level work with my useless degree. This is…life-changing, even if I only work there for a couple of years.

But more than the money, my curiosity overrides my trepidation and quite possibly my common sense. If I come this close to answers and then turn and walk away without even setting foot in the building and getting a *glimpse* of what I'm rejecting, how could I possibly live with that? I'd spend the rest of my life haunted by what could have been. Probably become one of those locals ranting and raving about various conspiracy theories and ghost radio channels in the middle of the night.

I take a deep breath, lean back in my chair, and raise my eyes to meet Dr. Wright's again. "Do you have a pen?"

Chapter Five

I've signed away a whole lot of rights in that NDA, but I'm still allowed to talk about the very basics, like the offer of a job as a "research tech" at the Facility. But I keep it to myself anyway. Part of me is afraid that if I tell my parents, they'll talk me out of it. Especially if I mention the strange circumstances of the offer—Dr. Wright showing up at the house after the questions I asked around town. They'll think it's sketchy…because it is. It really, really is. If I had any sense, I would probably be fleeing town, and quite possibly the country, right now.

Yet when Sunday night rolls around, I make up an excuse of a fake shopping trip with old friends to make sure I can have the car the next day, and my parents agree.

On Monday morning, I wake up, get ready, and drive toward the building that most of this town tries to ignore. The building that doesn't seem to exist according to any sources outside of Ash Valley.

My heart is pounding as I roll up to the security booth at the gate. The more I try to quiet my mind, the more it seems to babble on about mysterious disappearances, secret prisons, portals to hell, and all the other wild conspiracy theories I encountered when asking about this place. I have no idea what I'm about to walk into, or if it's dangerous.

But that's why I'm here, I remind myself. To find out once and for all what this place is. I take a deep breath and roll my window down.

The sour-faced, uniformed man within leans out to scrutinize me and the car. "Name?" he asks.

"Samara Vance," I answer.

He checks his computer and then squints at me. "ID."

I hand over the two forms that Dr. Wright instructed me to bring: my driver's license and my passport. The security guard spends an uncomfortably long time scrutinizing them and scanning them into his system before finally handing them back. Then, without a word from him, the gate opens.

Just like that, I'm entering the Facility. But my sense of awe quickly fades. Within the walls, the building is far less exciting than the imagination suggests. The grounds look like I would expect from any military facility—or prison, for that matter— nothing but dirt, a small parking lot, and the boxy, windowless building at the center. Whatever secrets this place has, they're beyond *those* walls, not the first set of electric fences.

After parking and heading to the only entrance I can see, I'm met by a blast of air conditioning and a second security guard. This one is a woman and just as cranky as the first. She asks me to hand over my cell phone and step through the kind of body scanner that I've only seen in airports.

After that, she takes my picture and hands over a security card and a lanyard. She stresses that the card is *temporary*, and honestly, thank God for that. The picture is terrible. I look wide-eyed and washed-out, grimacing because I wasn't sure whether I should look friendly or serious. From there, I'm ushered into a hallway where Dr. Wright herself is waiting for me. It's a relief to see a familiar face, even though it's a woman who scared the shit out of me last time we met.

"Welcome, Ms. Vance," she says, giving me a handshake. I smile at her, but she doesn't return it. Instead, she turns and sets off down the hallway. Feeling a bit like a kicked dog, I slink after the clack of her high heels. Her pace is brisk, not giving me much time to take in the building around me. But then again, there's not much to see. The tile and paint are all pure white, and the building is completely silent except for the sound of our footsteps. Harsh fluorescent lights render everything in sharp angles, and the air is uncomfortably cold, chilling my film of anxiety sweat from the ride over. Seemingly endless metal doors line each wall, each with their own security scanner.

All of the doors are closed and identical except for the numbered brass plates. They come in pairs—doors 1 and 1B, 2 and 2B, etc. I glance around as we go, eager for some hint of what I'm about to walk into, but get nothing.

The place feels weirdly empty. The other employees must be behind those closed doors, or sequestered elsewhere. At least that can put to rest one piece of my anxiety—the very mundane fear lurking behind all of the conspiracy theories: my dread of running into Ethan while I'm here.

Dr. Wright comes to a stop in front of the door numbered 13. *Ominous.* I suppress a nervous laugh.

"Try your security card and make sure it works," she says.

I fumble with the card around my neck before holding it up to the scanner. It takes a moment to think, then lets out an affirmative chirp and flashes a green light. At Dr. Wright's gesture, I reach for the handle and open the door.

A tiny box of a room awaits. There's a rectangular metal table that hosts an intimidating control panel and some screens, a single metal chair, and four blank walls.

"This," Dr. Wright says, "is Observation Room 13. If you accept the job, your role will be to record the behavior of subject X-13."

Nerves and curiosity twine in my gut. Maybe the *secret prison* theory was right. Maybe I'm here to observe some kind of high-level criminal—though for what purpose, I couldn't begin to guess at. "And who is this subject?" I ask, my eyes drifting toward the screens. But before I can get a good look, she leans over the desk and taps a button on the control panel.

"The correct question would be: *What* is this subject?" she says. As she speaks, the wall in front of the table slides open— turning out to be two panels instead of a solid wall—and reveals a window underneath, looking into an adjacent room that must be *13B*.

My breath hitches in surprise and wonder. There's something a little bit sci-fi about all of this; I've seen observation rooms used in psych experiments before, but nothing quite so high-tech. Rather than asking the question she's suggested, or letting my brain run wild with outlandish theories, I lean forward and peek through the window to see *what* exactly I'm going to be working with.

At first, I think that I'm looking at an empty room. There's only a small cot tucked in one corner, a plastic table, a chair, and smooth metal walls. I wonder if this is some kind of prank, a hazing ritual for new employees, or if they have yet to bring in my subject. But when I glance sideways at Dr. Wright, her expression is deadly serious; she doesn't seem like the type for jokes or wasting time. When she catches my questioning look, she leans forward and adjusts a lever on the panel, which increases the brightness in the room.

"Look more closely," she says.

I turn back to the cell, and something catches my attention. At first, my eyes gloss over it, assuming it's just a shadow. But something about it nags at me, and when I look back at the patch of darkness in the corner, I realize there's nothing in the room that would cast such a shadow. Nothing with those jagged edges.

A chill creeps up my spine. The feeling stirring in my chest is half fear and half awe. Once I notice it—as if in response— it ripples and changes; its edges blur and then settle into a new shape, rounded and soft. Another moment, and it peels away from the wall and bleeds into the center of the room, like a slow-spreading stain of darkness. Upon a closer look, it doesn't look like it's *on* the floor, but rather hovering slightly over it, like a murky cloud.

"Is that...?" I ask, a little breathlessly. I don't realize how far I'm leaning forward until my nose is almost against the glass, one hand hovering above it. I pull back with an embarrassed flush. I try to pay attention to Dr. Wright instead, but my eyes keep getting drawn back to that strange shadow.

"Yes," Dr. Wright says. "That is subject X-13."

"Is it *alive*?" I have no idea what to make of that thing, the strange, moving shadow. I've never seen anything like it, never even heard of such a thing except in horror stories. It looks... impossible. The way it moves and changes defies the world as I know it.

"To some extent, yes," Dr. Wright says. Her eyes track the slow movements of the subject and her expression is calm, like this is far from the weirdest thing she's seen today. Even though she's been working here for years, I can't imagine myself ever getting to a point where I could see something like this without any reaction whatsoever. "It shows responses to various stimuli such as sight, smell, sound, and touch. It has also made repeated attempts to escape its containment, which show a certain level of intelligence." My first thought is that I don't blame the thing; that cell looks utterly boring. But I brush that away and focus on Dr. Wright as she continues. "However, it has not shown any attempts at communication, or behavior that would indicate it has a higher degree of cognition than an average mammal."

I have *so* many questions I want to ask. Not only about this…creature I'm looking at, but about the other subjects they're researching here. As wild as some of the conspiracy theories were, they didn't suggest anything quite like this.

But after considering and tossing aside several various questions, concerns, and comments, I settle on the one that seems most pressing and relevant to my own line of work: "What *is* it, though?"

She looks as unsurprised by the question as she is by everything else. "If you work in this facility for very long, Ms. Vance, you will find that such a question is rarely easy to answer. Our work here focuses on subjects that we do *not* understand. Subjects that often stretch the bounds of what we consider to be logical and true about our very sense of reality."

"So you're saying… They're…" I feel foolish, but the word slips out anyway. "Monsters. You're studying monsters."

"That is a word for them, yes," she says, and the matter-of-fact tone makes the reality of the situation truly sink in. I grab the edge of the desk and squeeze hard enough that the pain helps convince me this is real. "We believe many of the subjects we hold here are the inspiration for various urban legends and myths around the world. But there is nothing mystical about them—we just do not understand them yet."

"O…kay." I raise a hand and press my fingers to my temple, trying to process this. "But where did it come from? And how does it…exist? And what *else* exists?"

Stern as she usually comes off, the way Dr. Wright looks at me is surprisingly sympathetic. "If I may give you one piece of advice, it would be to discard such questions. Focus on the concrete: what you can see and hear and record in data. Anything else is a distraction."

I nod. The words are kind—*ish*—but there is a darker underlying message: *don't ask too many questions. It is not your place to understand.*

However, after a moment, her features soften ever so slightly. She places a folder in front of me and flips it open to the first page. "However, for ease of communication, we have assigned this particular creature a moniker, as with all of the rest," she says. "You may refer to it as such." She taps a bold line typed at the very top of the first page. It reads "Subject X-13: *The Nightmare.*"

I mouth the words, my eyes locked on the file, but Dr. Wright shuts it before I can read more. When I look up at her, she lifts a brow at my obvious curiosity.

"Of course, anything more is classified," she says. "Unless you accept the job. And even if you do not, I must remind you that you can never speak a word about what you've seen here to the rest of the world, under penalty of law."

I blink at her, confused for a moment. But that's right. I told her I wouldn't officially accept until I understood more about the nature of the job. For a moment, I was so swept up in all of this that I almost forgot I didn't actually work here yet.

I press a hand to my lips and look through the window at the moving shadow again. *The Nightmare.* Maybe I should be intimidated by the name—scared at the idea of working with something so far beyond my understanding of the world. And I am, a little bit. I'm not a complete fool; it's obvious there's a lot more that Dr. Wright isn't telling me, and the name hints that the subject is not exactly easy to work with. Maybe not even *safe* to work with.

Yet at the same time... The thought of saying no, walking out that door, and living with this tantalizing bit of knowledge without speaking of it for the rest of my life is agonizing. I hoped that a visit to the building might sate my curiosity, and that the work here would turn out to be far less exciting than the rumors, making it easy to say no. And yet being here, seeing this thing, this *monster*, has raised more questions than it's answered. And I want to know more. I want to *understand.* I may die of curiosity if I deny myself that opportunity.

And I mean... I've always craved an adventure, haven't I? I've always lost myself in books and TV shows and dreamed of a world more exciting than the one I live in. Risky or not, how can I deny myself an opportunity like this when it drops into my lap?

With a decisive nod, I rip my eyes off the test subject, turn to Dr. Wright, and extend a hand.

"Dr. Wright," I say, "I would be delighted to accept your offer to work here. When can I start?"

Dr. Wright takes my hand. And, for the first time since I've met her, she gives me a genuine smile. "How does tomorrow sound?"

Chapter Six

The following day, I find myself in the observation room again, this time as an official employee of the Facility, or the Melsbach Research Facility, which I've learned is the official name of this place. Even within the building, nobody seems to use it—most people say MRF for short, and occasionally the more on-the-nose *Monster Research Facility*.

My excitement hasn't faded since my first visit. It takes all of my willpower to sit still in my observation chair. I can't take my eyes off the subject through the glass. The *Nightmare*, as they call it. I can't deny that the name is fitting—it looks like something out of one of my late-night terrors. Yet, at the same time, there is something mesmerizing about it. I could easily watch it all day, even if I weren't getting paid for it.

It's fascinating to observe its constant shifting movements, the way it seems to solidify into certain shapes before dispersing into a pool of shadow again. Even more intriguing, the screens showing different camera angles all seem to capture slightly different versions of it; its outline is even blurrier and undefined on a screen, and whenever it changes, the image goes pixelated and staticky, like a video game glitching.

I was all too eager to get my hands on the folder that Dr. Wright showed me a tantalizing glimpse of yesterday, but to my disappointment, it wasn't on the desk when I arrived. I found only a notebook for me to record observations in, with examples of how to structure my notes. I'm annoyed at the bait-and-switch, but there isn't anyone here to complain to, and even if there were, I probably wouldn't have the guts to do it.

I'm sure they'll be willing to give me more information once I prove that I'm reliable. So I dedicate myself to the task.

And it's not hard to focus on observation, anyway. I'm enthralled by the subject—the *Nightmare*, I keep thinking, with a tinge of something dangerously like awe—and I'm not sure I could stop watching it even if I tried. I have to keep reminding myself to stop and take notes, marking every time it changes its shape or drifts to a new location or does anything else that seems worth noting.

After a full day of observing the subject's behavior, I've taken note of a couple of the more frequent shapes it takes when it moves. The amorphous cloud seems to be its default, but it often shows longer tendrils that seem almost like ethereal tentacles, jagged lines like sharp teeth, and occasionally a crawling mass that seems like the shadow of a hundred human hands. The last one makes the hair on the back of my neck rise every time, but regardless, I'm more curious about the creature than frightened of it so far. Maybe I should be warier, but it hasn't shown any signs of aggression, and its movements are usually sluggish and aimless.

Still, I'm sure I wouldn't be half so bold without the bullet-proof viewing panel between us and heavy steel walls keeping it fully contained.

As the subject ripples and shifts again, I scratch down a note. *No discernible stimulus: shape change, spiral pattern. Held for approx. ten seconds, swirling slowly, before returning to default.*

I've been strictly instructed on the facility's protocol. All notes are to be taken by hand, and turned in to my supervisor at the end of the day. Nobody has explicitly said as much, but I expect that the only files are physical ones within the building itself. Nothing digital that might be hacked or leaked to the outside world. The building is a dead zone for Wi-Fi and cell service. Even if all employees weren't forced to surrender all technology upon entering, nothing would work within these concrete walls. The cameras dotting the corners of the halls are old-school, their footage undoubtedly stored on-site rather than in a cloud someplace. Same with the single camera in my observation room, situated so it views the back of my head and the panel in front of me.

They take security very seriously here, and I can't say I blame them for it. If anything about this place and the subjects it contains leaked to the outside world, people would lose their absolute shit.

And I say that having only seen *one* of the subjects. I can't even imagine what else is here. Monsters? Aliens? Things that go bump in the night? If this thing exists, I can't imagine what else might. Are vampires real? Werewolves?

As my mind wanders into the land of folklore and fairy tales, the door opens behind me. I flinch a little, sitting up straighter in my chair and trying to pretend I'm paying absolute attention to the subject, even though it's doing nothing other than hovering menacingly at the moment. Okay, "menacing" is just my own personal reading of its behavior, but still. It's hard to interpret it as anything else, especially when they call it the freaking Nightmare.

A tall, thin man who looks only a few years older than me enters the room and shuts the door behind him. He has a mop of dark hair and a pair of round wire-framed glasses, and he's wearing a button-up shirt and a bowtie. On some people, it would be an exhaustingly trite look, but he manages to make it look endearing.

I blink. "Hi," I say. And then, realizing that might not be the most professional response, I add, "Can I help you?"

"Hey. I'm Ezra. Ezra Bradford, lab tech." He reaches out a hand to shake, which I accept, and then smoothly hands me a folded piece of paper with his other hand. "Passing along instructions from Director Ramsey."

"Instructions?" I look at the paper in my hand like it's a live grenade. I may have started getting used to watching the thing in the cell, but the thought of having to interact with it floods me with an anxiety so intense, it makes me nauseous. "Um, I thought I was only supposed to observe and record…"

"Right, yes, you're new here," he says. "And your name is…?"

"Oh." I flush, realizing he introduced himself and I didn't return the favor. "Sorry. Mara. Vance."

"Pleasure to meet you, Sorry Mara Vance," he says with a tiny smile. The dad joke and his warmth help me relax. "I was an observer when I started, too. Sometimes instructions will come along from up top, asking you to check responses to certain stimuli. Nothing dangerous, no direct interactions or exposure to the subject. It's all just pressing buttons on your control panel." He points out the expanse of blinking lights in front of me.

"They'll produce effects within the cell, play sounds from the speakers, release scents, et cetera. All you have to do is hit a button and record the response."

"I see." I take a breath and look at the panel he's pointing at. Everything is clearly labeled: "sound 1," "sound 2," "scent 1," and so on. It looks simple enough, and I'm relieved to hear it doesn't mean I have to do anything to the subject myself. Even the thought of speaking directly to it gives me a bit of a chill, but this? I can handle this. "Okay, thank you."

"Good luck," he says, and shuts the door on his way out, leaving me alone again.

I unfold the paper and scan the short list. It is bulleted, concise, and clear. Still, I scan it a few times to ensure I have no questions before laying it flat on the table and moving on to the first step: *Record subject response to Sound 1.*

I reach out, my hand hovering over the button for a moment. It feels like I'm stepping over a threshold, in a way, involving myself more directly in the experimentation process. But that's ridiculous. All I'm doing is hitting a button. I summon my resolve, smack the button, and recoil my hand quickly, struck with a rush of adrenaline like I just sent a risky text.

I don't hear the sound that plays over the speakers in the room. There's a button that will let me hear inside, but I've been instructed to keep that function turned off so I can record "unbiased" notes about the subject's response without knowing about the stimulus presented within.

X-13 responds immediately and obviously. Its dark form ripples like a pond struck by a rock, and then shifts in an abrupt jolt of a motion, its edges going spiky and jagged. Its movement stops. It hovers in place, still and sharp-edged. I have the impression of a hedgehog or a pufferfish sending out its spines in a defensive action, bracing itself against some foe.

But that is exactly the kind of biased reaction I am not

supposed to have. I dutifully scratch down an entirely objective account of its response, mentioning only the cessation of movement and the change to its form. Then I wait five minutes, while the subject remains motionless and unchanging and my hand remains poised over the paper for any changes, before moving on to the second instruction.

I hit Sound 2, and the jagged protrusions slowly recoil back into the creature's main body. It goes round and soft around the edges again, but it still seems denser and more contained than before I began producing the stimuli. Almost like it's bracing itself for something. But that's, again, just me reading sentience into its behavior.

I press Sound 4.

The shadow spreads like ink spilling across the white tile, or dry grassland catching fire, the movement far more rapid than anything I've seen from it before. Black tendrils lick at the walls and climb up the glass in front of me. My heart rate picks up, despite my self-reassurances that the subject is entirely contained. The tendril slithers across the glass, rears back, and slams against it like a fist.

The *thump* is muffled, but still enough to make me jump; the control panel rattles in front of me. I push back on my rolling chair until I slam into the wall, one hand raised in front of my face as if to ward off a threat.

The Nightmare stands in front of the glass, its shadowy form molded the shape of a man: tall and spindly, stretched and sharply angular, its face smooth and blank but clearly humanoid.

A cold dread swirls in my chest before sinking down, down, into the pit of my stomach. And even though it's a one-way mirror, and it doesn't have eyes inside the swirling darkness, I *swear* I can feel it staring at me.

Chapter Seven

A sudden noise makes me jump—but it's just the bell for my lunch break. I laugh nervously, hit the button to shut the observation window, and take a moment to gather myself. This will be my first real chance to interact with my coworkers, and I don't want them to know how rattled I am. I head to the bathroom first, to dab sweat off my forehead and make sure I don't have any embarrassing pit stains. After a couple of minutes, I still can't get the image of the humanoid Nightmare out of my head, but at least I'm no longer in danger of a nervous breakdown.

Dr. Wright showed me the door to the break room but didn't bring me inside. When I enter, I'm surprised it's not bigger. I was envisioning a big, cafeteria-style space. Instead, it's just a room with three round metal tables, each with a handful of uncomfortable-looking chairs, along with a small kitchen area with a fridge, microwave, standard-issue coffee maker, and sink. A couple of windows provide a bland view of the parking lot, and the fluorescent bulbs make the whole area look washed-out and flat. I resist the urge to scrutinize all of the shadows in the room, just to make sure they're the correct size and shape, and instead focus on the coworkers I'm trying to make a good impression on.

Five other people currently occupy the room. One of them, to my great displeasure, is Ethan. I freeze for a moment as we make eye contact, terrified he's going to invite me over and I'll be obligated by politeness to go—but instead, he only gives me the tiniest nod before returning to his conversation. Somehow, that leaves me feeling even worse. I swallow hard and walk past him to the kitchenette, grabbing a cup of coffee and my lunch.

When I turn back to the tables, I hesitate again. Ethan is sitting with three men, who are all staring at him in a way that makes me feel like he's holding court. None of them glance in my direction. The second table—beside them—is empty, and the third is occupied by Ezra, who I met earlier. Indecision tears at me, but after a couple of moments, Ezra notices me and waves me over. I join him with a small sigh of relief. It's better than sitting alone, and the fact that he's the only person in the room *not* gazing admiringly at Ethan makes me inclined to like him.

"Mara, right?" he asks as I sip my coffee. It's pretty bad, but at least it's hot.

"Yep. How's it going, Ezra?"

"Just grand. Enjoying your first day?"

"It's certainly interesting," I say. Part of me is tempted to say more, but I'm not sure how much I'm allowed to talk about. I stall by taking a big bite out of my turkey-and-Swiss sandwich. While I'm chewing, the door opens, and another employee walks in. I light up at the sight of another woman—I wasn't exactly *uncomfortable* in a room full of only men, but I wasn't *comfortable* either—but she walks quickly to the fridge without a glance at anyone. Including Ethan, who immediately waves in a failed attempt to get her attention. She grabs something from the fridge and leaves again with her head down. Ethan lowers his hand and mutters something to one of his companions that makes him laugh a bit too hard.

I eye Ethan, and then the door the woman left from. I can't help but wonder what the story is there, but I'm not going to earn myself a reputation for gossip. Instead, I look at Ezra and say, "I'm surprised there aren't more of us here."

"Ah, well." He shrugs good-naturedly. "They stagger the lunches. I suspect they're not too fond of us having much time together."

Thinking of the odd hand-delivered note system, and how I've never run into anyone in the hallways, I suspect he's right. "Weird," I mutter, before I can censor myself.

Ezra grins. "Oh, believe me. That's the *least* weird thing about this place."

I suspect he's right about that too.

Chapter Eight

I'm still shaken by the time I get home. The subject remained as it was—uncannily human-shaped, uncomfortably close to the glass, and completely motionless—until the end of my shift. It refused to react to any further stimulus. As I neared the end of the day, rather than recording my overall notes in the observation room, I grabbed the folders and scurried out to the hallway. I finished my paperwork out there, with my back pressed against the door and my heartbeat gradually slowing. It was a breach of protocol, but I couldn't handle the thought of the Nightmare staring at me any longer.

There was something unnerving about it taking a human shape. It made me think of it differently. It made the thought of conducting experiments on it *feel* different. It was no longer something mindless, or even a kind of fascinating animal, but something that looked similar to me.

The shape of it lingers in the back of my mind. I keep thinking I see it out of the corner of my eye, standing on the side of the road as I drive home, silhouetted in my parents' window as I pull up. I grimace, take a few nervous puffs of my vape, and rub my eyes. I must be overtired and suffering from an adrenaline comedown. That's all. Even though it's still relatively early, I want to scarf down a quick meal and head to bed. But those plans are foiled when I walk inside to the smell of food cooking. The bright smell of tomato sauce, savory spices, and browning meatballs…must be my mom's spaghetti. The scent is practically thick enough to taste, and heavy with nostalgia, helping to ease my nerves.

"Perfect timing, honey!" my mom says, peeking out of the kitchen with a broad smile. "I'm almost done here, and your dad is taking a quick shower. I wasn't sure if you'd be home for dinner. I tried calling earlier, but your phone was off…?"

Aw, crap. Her questioning look reminds me that I still haven't had a conversation with my parents about my new job. I wanted to make the decision about taking the offer without any outside input, but it's not like I can hide it from them, since I'm living here.

"Sorry about that, but yeah, smells great," I say. "There's something I've been meaning to talk to you and Dad about, actually, once we're all sitting down." I catch her concerned look and quickly add, "Nothing bad!"

I channel my nervous energy into helping finish the spaghetti sauce while we wait for my dad. The kitchen smells delicious, though sticky with heat as the house's poor old AC unit struggles with both the heat outside and the stove. I'm sweating by the time the meal is on the tablet. Once it's all ready, I head back into the kitchen to pour myself a glass of wine, and then return to the table—only to see a tall, dark silhouette in the doorway across from me.

I yelp, wine sloshing out of my cup as I jump back, throwing up my free hand in an attempt to defend myself.

"Mara?" My dad's brow furrows as he steps into the light.

I let out a shaky breath, embarrassment heating my cheeks.

"Oh my gosh. You startled me." I force a laugh, trying to brush it off as a *whoops, silly me* moment instead of admitting—even to myself—that for one terrifying moment I thought the Nightmare followed me home from the lab. I managed to forget the stress of the day while I helped my mom, but now it's back and my stomach is in knots.

That nerve-wracking moment doesn't make what I have to say any easier. I stall for as long as I can, *mmm*-ing over the spaghetti and sipping my wine a bit too fast while pretending not to notice the expectant glances from my mom. But finally, my plate and glass are both empty.

"So." I clear my throat, toy nervously with my empty wineglass. "I wanted to share some good news with you both. I got a job! A local job, believe it or not."

"Oh, how wonderful, Mara!" My mom gushes immediately, obviously thrilled to keep me close to home. My dad agrees but looks more thoughtful, no doubt running through the limited local job opportunities for someone with a college degree.

"Yeah, I'm excited." My voice squeaks with nerves. "It's at the Facility, actually."

Silence. My mom's smile gains a frozen quality. The lines of concern on my dad's face deepen as he glances at the wine stain on my collar from my scare earlier.

"Obviously, I can't tell you much about what I'm doing there," I say, desperate to fill the quiet, trying to sound as enthusiastic as I can. "But it's interesting work, and I'm really excited about it." I stop there, hoping it's enough to get them on board with the idea.

My dad clears his throat and exchanges a look with my mom. "It's just…unexpected, that's all," he says. "But if you're happy, we're happy. Right, Enora?"

My mom's smile finally gets unstuck, and she nods a little too enthusiastically. "Of course. And honestly, anything that keeps you with us in Ash Valley is fantastic news!" She hesitates, fingers toying with her napkin. "And I'm sure it's not as bad as everyone says it is. But maybe we should…*not* tell the neighbors, for a little while. I'm sure you don't need rumors flying." Before I can even respond, her eyes widen with a new realization. "Oh, and you'll be working with Ethan! How lovely."

I grimace. "Yeah," I say, strained, and get to my feet. "Anyone want another glass of wine to celebrate?"

* * *

A couple hours later and two more glasses of wine deep, I finally retreat to my bedroom. The wine renders my thoughts pleasantly hazy, and the conversation with my parents went better than I expected. But the minute I'm alone, looking at my wine-stained shirt in the mirror and reliving that moment of panic earlier, unease shivers through me again. Dinner was a good distraction, but now I have to avoid looking too hard at dark corners, afraid my nerves will make visions of the Nightmare materialize again. And when I climb into bed and shut my eyes, that dark silhouette is waiting in my thoughts.

My dreams provide no escape. They are haunted by the same figure. In these dreams, instead of sitting in the observation room and looking in, I am inside, looking out at a dark shape on the other side. I bang my fists on the window and scream for my release, but that shadowy form only writes down their observations. In the way of dreams, I know what they're writing: *12:00: The subject screams. 12:01: The subject screams. 12:02: The subject screams.*

I wake, drenched in sweat, to the blaring of my alarm. I slap it off and drag a hand across my face with a groan. It feels as though I haven't slept a wink—but no matter. It's my second day of work, and way too early to screw it up by being late. So I rush through a quick shower, get myself ready for the day, and head to the Facility.

* * *

My pulse is already rising as I cross through security and think about sitting in that room again. Every clack of my heels on the tile accelerates the drumbeat of my heart. When I step into my room, I nearly shriek as I realize someone is sitting in my chair.

"Oh, God," I say, laughing nervously. "You scared me!"

At least this is slightly more justified than getting startled by my own father. The sight of a sleazy ex-boyfriend sitting in their work chair would be enough to freak anyone out, right? Ethan smiles at me, holding a familiar file in his hand. "Good morning to you, too, Mara." He gestures to the file. "Your notes…"

I think of my breach of protocol yesterday, on my *first* day, and how ridiculous I'll sound trying to explain why I felt the need to cower out in the hallway. My stomach sinks. The first day was probably a test of my ability to stave off fear, and I failed. "Yes?" I ask, barely a whisper.

He sets the file down. "They're good. Thorough. Exactly what we like to see. Keep it up."

I'm not sure if I feel relieved or annoyed. At least I've not been doing anything wrong…but at the same time, who is he to come in and tell me that? Come to think of it, I don't know what position he holds here. With Ethan, it's hard to tell if he has some kind of authority, or if he's just being his usual smug self. Either way, he's looking at me like he expects a response, so after a moment, I manage a terse, "Thanks."

"So…following in my footsteps, huh?" He smiles as he says it, but it feels like an accusation. My stomach twists as I remember all the things he said about me after our breakup, that I was clingy, delusional, obsessed with him. My words stick in my throat, but after a pause, he continues, "I was surprised to hear you took the job. It can be pretty stressful, you know? Like I warned you. And you've always been so…sensitive."

Annoyance flares in me. He's *well* aware that word was the beginning of a hundred arguments between us back when we dated. He threw it at me every time I got upset—right until he swapped to *crazy*. I swallow back my knee-jerk reaction and force a smile. "I've done a lot of work on myself," I say. And it's *true*. I spent years in therapy, fixing the damage he did to me, but I'm not going to tell him that part. "I'm confident I can handle this opportunity, and I'm excited for it."

I don't know how he manages to make a smile look so condescending, but goddamn, he is good at it. "Well, I wish you the best of luck," he says. "Just let me know if you're having any problems, okay?"

"Of course." *Fat fucking chance.*

He takes the folder on his way out, leaving behind an empty log to fill for today. I sink into the chair slowly.

Annoying as it was, that conversation was almost a welcome

distraction, given how much I've been dreading this moment. I haven't been able to forget X-13's humanoid form, and the way it lurked close to the glass like it sensed me here. But now, as I raise my eyes to the window, it's doing nothing of the sort.

The Nightmare is in the top of the far corner of its cell, forming a hazy, vaguely spidery shape. It clings to the ceiling and walls with waving tendrils of shadow. It eases my anxiety, to see it farther away and no longer so human-shaped. Something about that really unnerved me; it made me feel like it knew I was here.

Now that I'm here again, I'm doubting whether it was ever exactly humanoid at all. Maybe I was afraid and read into its shape in my fear. I'm struck by the desire to look back over my notes from yesterday and reassure myself that I saw what I saw, but I can't. Ethan took them. And there's no point, anyway. The notes are not for me to reassure myself of my own memory, and I'd sound like a lunatic asking to look over them the next morning when Ethan already OK'd them.

As the day proceeds, my anxiety bleeds away. I haven't been asked to provide any stimulus, and the subject isn't behaving any differently than it did yesterday before it changed shape. It occasionally drifts and shifts, and sometimes an eerily humanlike arm or face will emerge from its swirling darkness. But it always melts away soon after, and it never forms anything resembling a person or tries to approach the viewing window again.

Then the slot on my door opens and a folded piece of paper drops onto the floor. I stare at it for a moment before scooting my chair over to grab it. More instructions await within, just like on the slip that Ezra handed me yesterday. I'm guessing this is the normal method of receiving orders from up high.

Yesterday must have been a special case because it was my first day and Ezra wanted to introduce himself.

I take a deep breath, bracing myself. Then, one by one, I go through the instructions and record the responses.

Sound 2: the subject twitches, but then gives no noticeable responses.

Scent 3: the subject wanders around the room—searching for something?—then settles in the middle of the room and idles.

Temperature increased, five degrees: no response.

Sound 3—

As soon as I hit the button to toggle the stimulus, the Nightmare's amorphous cloud turns jagged and spiky, swirling in a way that is difficult to interpret as anything other than distress. As I start to record its response, it suddenly flings itself at the barrier between us and hits the glass with a loud *thump*. I jump in my chair, dropping my pen, and stare wide-eyed as it retreats and then launches itself at the barrier again. *Thump*. I flinch back, instinctively rolling my chair away from my desk.

It seems…upset? Maybe it's wrong to attribute feelings to the thing inside the cell, but it's hard not to as I watch it flail and shift and make desperate attempts to free itself from its confinement. Guilt and worry gnaw at my stomach. Did I do something wrong? It's never reacted to other stimuli like this before.

Just when I think I can't possibly take it throwing itself at the barrier again, it collapses to the floor. It melts into a shape similar to a chalk outline of a human, and its surface becomes oddly matte and more solid than before. It stops moving.

Oh God. OhGodohGod. What have I done? Did I kill it?

Even if it's supposedly not intelligent or emotive, even if I was just following orders, the idea makes my chest tighten. At first, I was worried about getting in trouble, but now I'm more concerned that I've accidentally done something terrible.

I stand up to get a better look at the subject. It's still not moving, not even floating. It's lying motionless on the floor like a normal, everyday shadow. "Shit," I mutter, and then run my eyes and hands over the various controls on the panel. I *know* Dr. Wright pointed out an emergency alert button, but I can't remember which one it was. Instead, I find a switch that reads *Intercom Output*. When I hit it, noise begins to pour through the speakers. I flinch at the high-pitched screech, resisting the urge to slam my hands over my ears.

Then, having a lightbulb moment, I fumble and toggle off the *Sound 4* stimuli I had activated at the start of this. The high-pitched sound cuts off as soon as I do.

Guilt racks me all over again. No wonder the subject was so distressed by that noise. I run a shaking hand through my hair, sucking in a breath, and then impulsively swat at the *Intercom Input* switch.

"I'm sorry!" I blurt out, leaning over the mic on the desk. I feel silly doing this. *Obviously* this thing isn't intelligent enough to understand speech, but I can't fight a desperate desire to absolve myself, and a hope that maybe it will at least understand my tone well enough to know that I'm apologetic. "I didn't mean to hurt you, okay? I'm sorry. Please be okay."

For a moment, there's no response from within the cell. No motion, no noise. But then a clawed, five-fingered hand emerges from the puddle of shadow and grips the floor beside it.

Slowly—as if it is pulling itself out of a hole—the shadow

morphs and rises into a humanoid form. It's fuzzy around the edges, its shape indistinct, as if drawn by a shaky hand. Still, like yesterday, it is clearly recognizable as an attempt at a human body, albeit a nearly seven-foot-tall and stretched one. Its torso is too thin, its arms and neck too long, its head tilted at an angle that would be distinctly painful on a person and its "face" smooth and blank and eyeless.

Yet it is impossible to fight the sensation that it is trying to peer through the window at me. Again.

I'm still standing at my desk, frozen. It is somehow both creepy and fascinating, watching it imitate a human like this. Does it…understand that there's a person on the other side of the glass? Is that why it's doing this? A weird thought, but not impossible.

Of course, the idea that it's doing this because it understood me *is* impossible. Right? But I feel a weird thrum of uncertainty in my chest, staring at the Nightmare now. Surely it's just the evolved human sense of empathy at work here, but I can't help but view the subject differently when it appears more humanoid.

Before I can do anything more, the bell rings for my lunch break. I stay frozen in place for a few moments, tempted to work through it—but that will only gain me more attention, and I'm pretty sure I'm not supposed to be doing what I just did. So I quickly turn off the intercom toggle, tear myself away from my desk, and head to the break room.

* * *

This lunch is much the same as yesterday: Ethan ignores

me, and I sit with Ezra. I probably should be cultivating friendships, but it's hard to think of anything except for my subject right now. Our interactions play in my mind while I try to determine if it really was significant, or if I'm just seeing what I want to see. I barely speak a few sentences as I tear through my lunch, eager to get back to work. Ezra lifts an eyebrow at me but doesn't probe; I'm guessing you learn quickly not to ask too many questions in a place like this.

When I return to the observation room, my curiosity feels worse instead of better. X-13 is still standing right on the other side of the glass, the skinny fingers of one humanoid hand resting against the window. I can't suppress the growing temptation to try to communicate with it further, if only to reassure myself that it really didn't *actually* understand me. If anything, it must just be familiar with the sound of human speech and reacting to that. Surely it's worked with other humans before.

But surely it can't hurt to experiment a little more.

Even though I feel foolish, I toggle the intercom again. "Do you...understand me?" I ask, nearly a whisper, embarrassed that I'm even asking.

The shadow's head gradually tilts until it sits upright on its skinny neck. Then, slowly and distinctly, it nods.

I recoil from the control panel, pressing a hand to my chest as if trying to restrain my pounding heart. Oh God. Oh *shit*. There's nothing ambiguous about that response.

Or is there? I shut my eyes to close off its eerily humanoid form and try to let my rational brain take over. I run through what I know about experimenter bias and investigator effects. It's a known problem that scientists can accidentally affect their subjects and alter the results of an experiment. My perception is certainly colored by the fact it *seems* more human to me now.

I know very little about what I'm dealing with. This could be a type of creature designed to imitate other species and elicit empathy as some kind of defense mechanism. Cats evoke crying babies with the sounds they make in order to appeal to human nurturing instincts, but that doesn't mean they're superintelligent, manipulative geniuses. They've just evolved alongside humans. Same with horses and such that can do math, but they're really just responding to subtle cues from their handlers. This could be a similar case.

I let out a long, slow breath, calming myself. I can't rule anything out yet. Dr. Wright told me this subject *wasn't* intelligent…but it's possible that she and the others in the Facility don't fully understand it. Or that they're hiding something from me. I can't make any assumptions right now, but I feel obligated to perform some of my own research to find out more. I'd be a fool not to; I'm the one who's going to be working with this thing every day.

I open my eyes, focusing again on that odd, uncanny human shadow waiting on the other side of the glass.

My heart bangs out a nervous beat, and I'm hyperaware of the camera watching the back of my head right now. I know I've only been here for a few days, and I really shouldn't be diverting from the instructions I've been given…but they didn't explicitly tell me *not* to otherwise interact with the subject, did they? They only told me to make sure I check off everything on the list by the end of the day, and I've done that.

Plus, I didn't try to hide my actions earlier from the camera, and so far, no one has showed up to reprimand me. So there are two possibilities: either they're observing me and they don't care that I spoke to the subject, or they're not watching me closely at all. That would explain why nobody confronted me about my minor breach in protocol yesterday. I picture a bored security officer, who *surely* has more interesting things to watch than a nervous new employee and possibly-sentient shadow in this place, and relax a bit. They're paranoid about leaving evidence here, too—it's very possible these are cameras that only broadcast live and don't actually store recordings.

And if my suspicion about the subject behind the glass happens to be right…it'd be worth a small risk, because it could change everything. There's no way I could continue to work here in good conscience, if they're experimenting on intelligent beings in this place, rather than mindless monsters like they say they are. How can I live with myself if I don't at least try to make sure?

I scan the control panel until I find the one I'm looking for. *Privacy screen toggle*. That has to be what keeps me hidden from the subject. My finger hovers over it for a moment, my breath catching in my throat, before I hit it with a decisive jab.

There's no change on the window from this side. But judging from the way the subject twitches, its blank "face" turning in my direction, I suspect the button did exactly what I thought it would. It let the subject see me, standing here, on the other side of the glass.

I get out of my chair and force my trembling legs to move me closer. As close to the glass as I can get. The Nightmare moves on the other side and bends its giant form down until its face is near mine, separated only by the clear pane of the window.

I swallow hard, raise a shaking hand, and press it against the glass. With the other, I press down on the button to transmit my voice inside. "Hi," I breathe. "I'm… I'm Samara." The cloud ripples and then forms a vague impression of a face. *My* face, I realize with a jolt. I smile, and the imitation of my face mirrors the expression.

"That's right. That's me. I, um… I wanted to say I'm sorry for earlier. It seemed like I upset you."

My face dissolves, and the Nightmare twitches. A few spiky tendrils grow out of its shoulders and hips, imitating the way it looked when it threw itself at the glass earlier.

"Yes, like that," I say. A sense of wonder comes over me. "You really can understand what I'm saying, can't you?"

The Nightmare lifts one mostly human hand—much larger than mine, ending with curved claws—and presses against the other side of the glass. Its head slowly nods, the motion smoother this time. Like it's learning alarmingly quickly how to imitate me…or remembering how to be humanoid.

We stay there for a moment. It says nothing, does nothing else, but I feel in my bones that my growing suspicion is right. The things Dr. Wright told me about this subject are not true. It is no mindless monster, or sentience akin to "an average mammal." It is intelligent, and capable of communication, and just as able to think and feel as I am.

So what does that mean for me?

* * *

At home, I can't stop thinking about subject X-13. The Nightmare. I stay up late, curled in bed and scrolling through endless Wikipedia pages on my phone, trying to learn more about the nature of the monster that I'm studying. Dr. Wright did mention that many of the creatures in the Facility have inspired folklore and urban legends, so surely there must be something out there.

What I find is not encouraging. I end up falling into an endless abyss of new tabs, reading about night terrors and sleep paralysis, demons and shadow people and aliens and djinn. I stare with bloodshot eyes at a painting called *The Nightmare*, momentarily paralyzed by the sight of a horrifying creature crouched on a helpless woman's chest.

Finally, I tear my eyes away, shut my phone off, and force myself to lie down.

It takes a long, long time to fall asleep. And when I do, I dream again about the Nightmare.

I'm lying in my bed as its lanky humanoid silhouette looms over me. I try to sit up, to speak, to do *anything*, but I can't do more than twitch my fingers and my eyes. The Nightmare leans over me, looking down into my face with its blank one, and terror claws at the inside of my chest. I try to writhe or scream, but I can't. My heart pounds in my ears, and my eyes frantically move back and forth, while the rest of me is paralyzed. A bead of sweat rolls down my forehead and stings my eye, and all I can do is blink it away, breath shuddering.

The figure leans closer, closer, until its shadowy void of a face is only inches from mine. I catch a whiff of something smoky and spicy. A huge hand lifts over my cheek, the tips of curved claws trailing just over my skin. Then the darkness splits into a jagged mouth, and it whispers in a deep, gravelly voice that reverberates in my bones: *"Samara."* The sound of my name in its mouth, its faceless attention focused on me, makes me want to run. But I can't move. It leans in even closer, claws drawing close to my skin and its mouth nearing my ear as it whispers, *"Let me out."*

A claw pricks my face, and I scream.

* * *

I sit up, heart pumping, body slick with sweat under my tangled sheets. The Nightmare is gone, but my eyes rove the room as my chest heaves, sure I'm about to find it hiding in a corner, or my closet. I even look up at the ceiling just to make sure.

It takes me a good thirty seconds to realize I'm awake now, and another minute to calm down my panicking body.

It seemed so *real.* I can still feel the lingering pain where its claw cut into my skin. But what really unnerves me is that there was no clear moment where I went from asleep to awake. Even now that the haze of sleep is clearing from my mind, I feel uncertain. Confused.

It must have been sleep paralysis. That's why I couldn't move; my body was still locked in a dream even though I was half awake. I learned all about such episodes in my studies in the sleep lab at university, though I've never experienced one myself. But still, even as I rationalize it, there's a rock of unease sitting heavily in my stomach.

It's nearly time to wake for work, anyway, so I drag myself out of bed and into the shower. The water washes off my nightmare sweat, and the warmth eases the cold out of my bones. I feel better when I climb out, but then I look into the mirror and frown, swiping a hand across it to clear the fog and take a better look.

There, right on my cheekbone where the Nightmare touched

me in my dream, is a small red mark.

Chapter Nine

It's hard to act normal at my observation desk after the terrifying dream I had last night. The mark on my face burns—though I know it must just be a bug bite that sparked the dream, or a place I absently scratched in the shower, it still has me rattled.

There is a war of sensations within me as I watch the Nightmare through the observation window. Suspecting that it's a great deal more intelligent than I was told, I feel bad that it's trapped within such a tiny room with so little stimulation, forced to run through boring tests like some kind of lab rat. But I'm also shaken up after that nightmare, and afraid of coming face-to-face with it again, even through the safety panel.

But I'm being ridiculous. It was just a dream. This—even though it feels equally as surreal—is real life. And real life has its own problems to deal with.

Namely, X-13. I'm already starting to question my last interaction with it. Is it possible the subject was just imitating me, and I was tricked? Or, even if it can understand speech to some degree, how smart *is* it? Dogs and dolphins and apes can understand some words, too, but that doesn't place them anywhere near a human's level of intelligence.

But if it *is* intelligent, like my gut suggests it is… Then what? Did Dr. Wright lie to me, or does she have no clue about the subject's true nature?

There are too many questions. If the subject does prove to be intelligent, I'll need to do something about it—whether that's quitting my job, advocating for better treatment, or what, I'm not sure yet. But first, I need to be damn sure I'm right. Even more than that, I need to have evidence that Dr. Wright and the other higher-ups will respect. And in order to collect evidence, I need to run some tests of my own, without slacking on my normal day-to-day work and getting myself fired before I can find out the truth.

It's a bit daunting to think about, but it's also thrilling. *This* is the kind of thing I'd hoped to be doing within the Facility, the kind of thing I've always dreamed of doing in some way: making discoveries, uncovering secrets of the mind and the universe. Changing the world.

I never thought it might involve a secret monster research facility and a sentient shadow, but honestly? I can't complain.

So, after racing through the day's instructions as quickly as possible and jotting down the requisite notes, I decide to use the hour or so I have left to run some of my own tests. I take down the privacy screen and just like yesterday, the Nightmare comes up to the glass the moment I do. It imitates my face again and then presses a clawed, shadowy hand against the glass, just like before.

I smile, pressing my hand against the pane between us. Maybe I should be terrified by the size of the Nightmare's hand in comparison to mine, and the curved claws—and I do feel a tingle of fear, remembering the nightmare I had about it last night—but mostly I feel excited at yet another display of intelligence. "That's right. You remember."

It taps a claw against the glass, almost like it's asking for something, but I'm not sure what. But it does remind me uncomfortably of my dream, and I have to swallow back a burst of fear and suppress the urge to step away. I'm not going to punish a real, possibly intelligent being because of a bad dream.

"I want to run a few baseline tests today," I say. The Nightmare tilts its head but doesn't otherwise respond, so I carry on. "First, some basic questions..."

I'm hesitant to write any of this down before I'm ready to talk to my superiors, so I have to go from memory and trust my own observations. It's possible they're watching me over the security camera anyway, but I haven't been confronted about it yet, so either they haven't noticed, or they don't care. Either way, I doubt the camera can pick up my quiet words, so they'll probably see no more than me standing at the observation window.

The subject doesn't speak. It only nods or shakes its head yes or no, but still, its answers seem logical and clear.

Do you understand what I'm saying? A nod.

Are you comfortable being questioned by me? Another nod.

Do you understand that I am human? Once again, a yes.

Do you consider yourself *human?* A side-to-side shake.

Are you aware that you are trapped here? Nod.

Are you happy here? Another vehement *no*.

Can you speak? It hesitates, uncertain, like it isn't sure how to answer.

I'm about to ask more but am cut off at the sound of the slot on the door opening again. I whirl guiltily to see another envelope plop on the floor.

I've never received two envelopes in one day before. Do they know I finished early? Are they watching me more closely than I suspected?

I open the envelope, fearing some kind of reproach within, but instead, it's just another set of instructions. For a moment, I feel a twinge of suspicion. Did they notice what I'm doing after all? Are they trying to prevent me from doing my own tests to check the intelligence of the subject? No, I decide. Surely they would've confronted me directly if they did. They must just assume I've gotten used to my routine and can handle more tasks. If anything, I take this as further confirmation that they're *not* keeping a close eye on me.

I return to my desk with the new set of instructions. The Nightmare is still standing on the other side in human form, like it's waiting for me to talk to it again. "Sorry," I say, realizing the intercom is still activated. "Back to our regularly scheduled programming, I'm afraid." I shut off the intercoms and then turn the privacy screen back on to hide me from the subject.

The subject slams a fist against the glass. I jump and then sigh under my breath as it does it again, and then starts pacing with irritation. It's like a dog upset that a training session is over. Or a child throwing a temper tantrum.

Or a conscious being reasonably angry that it's been cut off from its only form of meaningful communication, a small voice in the back of my head whispers. But I tell it to quiet down. I still don't know enough to make assumptions…and, more importantly, I have a job to do.

"I did say sorry," I mutter as I reach to hit the button for *Sound 1*.

Still, I can't fight off a wave of guilt as I start going through the mind-numbingly boring stimulus tests again, while the subject sulks and refuses to respond on the other side.

* * *

The Nightmare appears again when I fall asleep. This time, it is angry.

I know, with the small portion of rationality that I cling to in my dreams, that this must be a manifestation of my guilt over work today. This Nightmare in my brain is just a cobbled-together version of the angry responses I've seen from its real version. And this is just a dream.

But that doesn't stop me from being fucking terrified as it looms up over my bed.

It draws itself up taller—and taller, and taller, bones cracking and limbs bending at strange angles, until its head scrapes the ceiling and its limbs and body are stretched long and thin and disjointed. The proportions are all wrong, but its face is the worst. Features are starting to form instead of its usual blank mask, but they are all wrong, its eyes too big and its mouth too wide. Its smile stretches like its body did. Its lips pull back to reveal a snarl of too many teeth, spread from ear to ear, covering half of its face. A long, long tongue slips out between the rows of fangs and licks at the air like it's tasting my fear.

"Just a dream," I whisper to myself. "Just a dream, just a dream..." But my voice goes higher and squeakier with each repetition, and when the ghoulish form lunges towards me again, I scream and fling myself out of bed.

I hit the floor hard. The pain jolts me, and for a moment I think I must have woken up—but the Nightmare is still here, grinning that ghoulish grin from the other side of the bed, so I must still be dreaming. I scramble to my feet and sprint for the door. Outside is the hallway of my parents' house, just like in real life. As I run, it becomes longer and longer, the floorboards moving like an escalator under my feet. Behind me, the Nightmare floats across the floor, a dark cloud of tendrils and claws reaching for me. I swear and stumble onward, pushing myself until I finally reach a door, but when I open it and fling myself through, I'm back in my bedroom.

"No, no," I sob. I turn to run again, but one clawed hand is already gripping the doorway from the other side. It bends to look through the door, neck snapping to the side with a hideous crack, horrible grin leering in at me. It grabs the sides of the doorway, claws scraping against wood, and starts to pull itself through.

Struck with a childish desperation, I fling myself to the floor and crawl toward the bed. Maybe I can hide beneath it. Maybe it's too big to fit there—

Then I reach the edge of my bed, one hand extended underneath. Too late, I realize the darkness beneath the mattress is too deep, too solid. Too late, I see a gleam of eyes.

The Nightmare is already waiting for me under the bed, and before I can recoil, claws close around my wrist and drag me underneath, into the darkness with it. I writhe, trying to free myself, but it's all around me now. A warm, living shadow that envelops me, trapping me, tearing at my pajamas and creeping across my skin, flooding my senses with a smoky scent. Dark laughter echoes in my ears, and all over my body I feel gripping fingers, slithering tentacles, spider legs and teeth and a slavering tongue—

I scream, hoping I'll wake myself, but a hand clasps over my mouth and stops me.

I can't *breathe*. I should always be able to breathe, it's a dream, a fucking dream, and you can always breathe in a dream even when you plug your nose; it's a way to know you're dreaming. But I *can't*.

Am I strangling myself with my covers? Is it possible to scare yourself to death?

I thrash and struggle, to no avail. I can't move an inch with the shadows clinging to me, slowly tightening like a boa constrictor covering my entire body at once. It *hurts*.

Maybe I should give up. Let the darkness take me—

But no. No. I refuse. I will not die in my bed of fear like a fucking idiot in this fucking stupid town. I will not let my parents find my body in the morning. I will not die before I've even been able to live. I'm not *done*.

My terror turns, suddenly and fiercely, to anger. The scream of fear turns into a shriek of rage, and I bite down *hard* on the shadowy hand over my mouth. It writhes, trying to escape, but I only clamp down harder and grind my teeth, until I feel the surface break and something warm and salty fills my mouth. Then I spit it out and scream, *"Fuck you!"*

* * *

I wake up, breathing in short, hard gasps, in my bed. The scent of smoke lingers in my nose and mouth. The comforter is twisted all around me, tangled up around my neck, and I swear and flail in rage until I manage to disentangle myself and shove it off the side of the bed. Once it's gone, I sit up, raking a hand through my sweaty hair, and glare down at the pile of fabric on the floor.

"Fuck you," I mutter at it again. "Not today, motherfucker. Not ever, not like that."

Then I put my face in my hands, let out a low groan, and wonder how hard it would be to get an Ambien prescription.

Chapter Ten

Later that morning, I arrive at work to find a considerably longer list of tasks waiting on my desk. Again, I feel a flicker of uncertainty. Is this a punishment for diverging from my instructions, or are the higher-ups just giving me more work now that I'm getting the hang of this? Either way, there's no chastisement over my interactions with the subject. Surely, if I were doing something wrong, someone would let me know. So I take their silence as approval.

But today, it seems I'll barely have time to do the tests they're requiring me to run, let alone enough to get creative with my own. Especially given that I'm utterly exhausted.

Honestly, I'm relieved that I won't have to be face-to-face with the Nightmare after that horrible dream last night. Just looking at it through the observation panel makes the hair on the back of my neck stand on end.

At first, I sit rigid and tense in my chair, nervous every time I have to take my eyes off the subject and check my instructions again. I keep expecting to look up and see that horrible, sharp-toothed grin pressed against the glass. But as the hours drift by and nothing interesting happens, my adrenaline fades and exhaustion takes its place. Soon enough, I find myself struggling not to nod off in my chair.

But every time I find my eyes starting to slide shut, I remember that dream—the terrible grin, the hand clamping over my mouth—and snap back awake to glare at the Nightmare in its cell.

I know it's not the subject's fault that I'm having nightmares about it. Not really. Still, I can't fight the resentment or the sense that these horrible dreams are punishing me, somehow. Maybe my brain is punishing itself. But what have I done to deserve this? I'm working on proving the subject's intelligence when I can, and otherwise, I'm following instructions. Doing my job. The *only* job available to me in this washed-up little town.

But no matter how much I try to justify it to myself, the guilt remains.

* * *

At lunch, I pick at my food and drain two terrible cups of coffee, longing for the creative flavors of Cup o' Happy. Ezra watches me with a concerned furrow between his brows.

"You feeling all right?" he asks.

"Yeah, yeah." I flutter a hand in a half-hearted gesture. "I just…well. You know."

It's a vague answer, but he nods like he does understand. "The first week is the hardest," he says. "After that, it gets…" He hesitates. "Well, you get used to it. You'll be surprised to see that a job like this can get *boring*, but trust me, it does."

I smile wanly. "Wow. Quite the pep talk."

"Would you prefer some cheesy inspirational quotes? Perhaps printed over delightful images of the beach? Because I could ask about putting some up in here..."

It feels impossible to laugh after the day I've had, but somehow I'm doing it anyway. "Oh, God, please no. Anything but that."

Ezra laughs along with me but quiets rather abruptly, glancing across the room. I follow his gaze to find Ethan staring at us. He looks away as soon as I catch his eye, turning his back to us.

I groan, sinking down in my chair. "Of all the people to share a lunch break with," I mutter.

Ezra raises his eyebrows, leaning forward. "Have you already got beef with Mayhew?" he asks, voice lowered and eyes bright with curiosity. "I mean, not that I blame you. Dude thinks he's so *very* high and mighty, even though the director only favors him for his local connections."

I file that information away for later as I huff a laugh under my breath. "Oh, I realized he was an asshole *long* ago. We dated. Unfortunately."

"Oof."

"Yup. I'm sure you can imagine." I roll my eyes and suck a breath through my teeth.

"Not sure I want to."

We share another laugh; I press a hand to my mouth in an attempt to muffle the sound and avoid Ethan's ire. When I realize Ezra is doing the same, it sends us both into near hysterics. When lunch is over, I'm relieved to feel I have something akin to a friend here—but when I return to the observation room, it's just me and the Nightmare, once again.

* * *

The Nightmare is waiting when I fall asleep. I'm curled up beneath the covers, glaring up at it while it stands at the foot of the bed.

Though his form bleeds around the edges like a blurry photograph, he holds one shape, and looks even more humanoid this time, so much so that I find myself mentally using *him* instead of *it* because there is a clear masculinity to his shape. His build is lean rather than bulky, but he still has broad shoulders and a tapered torso that makes me think of defined muscles. And his face is getting clearer too. Moonlight illuminates sharp features and dark eyes that watch me unblinkingly.

The atmosphere is different from the other nightmares I've had. It doesn't feel like he's trying to frighten me. He stands still at the end of my bed, keeping his distance, almost like he's trying *not* to scare me.

Instead, he's looking at me like he's trying to figure me out.

I stare back, studying him too. And the more I do, the more I sense a strange allure to his inky darkness.

It's probably a screwed-up thing to think about, especially after the terror of my last nightmare. He's a figure made of pure shadow, with sharp teeth and sharper claws. *And* a dream figment of the creature I'm studying at work in my daytime hours. I wonder what this says about my psyche. Is it a manifestation of the guilt I'm feeling? Is my brain picking up on the Nightmare's more human characteristics and creating a dream version of him that I can relate to?

Then again, I've always been the kind of freak who is weirdly turned on by monster movies. Maybe it's nothing deeper than that. And either way, so what?

This is just a dream. It's not like it matters. Nobody will judge me for whatever happens in my own mind. So what if I'm thinking about those huge hands and that long tongue from my last dream? The way he changed shapes and all of the possibilities that could entail?

I flush as my mind wanders down a dirty path, and the way the Nightmare tilts his head in scrutiny makes me feel like he can sense my thoughts. His form flickers, and then he's abruptly closer to me, sitting on the edge of my bed rather than standing alongside it. I swallow hard, fighting back a pulse of mingled fear and desire, and pull the blankets tighter. This seems like a good dream, not a nightmare, but I still feel vulnerable.

"Mara," the Nightmare says, like he's trying it out. His voice is low and smooth, with a whispery quality that makes me shiver in a not-entirely-unpleasant way. Christ, what is wrong with me?

"X-13," I say in return, barely a whisper. But it sounds strange, wrong. I bite my lip. "Nightmare?" I try, but that doesn't feel right either. "Do you have a name?" I ask, finally.

"Many," he responds, but doesn't offer any.

I sit up in bed. This close, with moonlight streaming through the window, I can make out more of his features. The curve of a shapely nose, and prominent cheekbones; eyes framed by thick lashes, and full lips; all formed by a strange sort of darkness that shimmers faintly where the light hits it. Shadowy tendrils with the texture of hair drift across his forehead and cheeks, floating as if stirred by a nonexistent wind. Everything about his features is a little too sharp to feel properly human—not even counting the claws and the teeth—and his form is still too long, lean and wispy and ethereal. Something is a little *off* in a way that's unsettling to the eye, but he's eerily beautiful in its own way. I find myself studying his face, wondering at the texture of his hair.

Of course my dreams would make the Nightmare hot. Blurring the monster that occupies most of my waking hours and all of my repressed, lonely desires into one. I bite back a laugh at the absurdity of my own brain. But if my mind wants to offer up weird, horny fantasies instead of nightmares, well, I'll happily take it. And it is *just* a dream, after all.

Emboldened, I sit up and reach out to touch the Nightmare's arm. He stays still as my fingers reach his shadowy "skin." I expect them to pass through like he's nothing more than smoke or find a chilling cold. Instead he's velvety soft, and warm, and solid. When I don't pull away, he mirrors my motions with his other arm, touching me the same way I'm touching him. Though it's still impossible to read his shadowy features, I feel like he's experiencing the same fascination as I am. Like my human body is as interesting to him as his shadowy one is to me. His fingers drift up over the slope of my shoulder, to the curve of my neck, and I find myself leaning back to expose the column of my throat to him—

* * *

I wake with a gasp and stare up at the ceiling for a few seconds as the dream lingers in my mind…along with a pulsing ache between my thighs. But close on its heels comes a sense of crawling shame. How sexually frustrated do I have to be in order to dream about my monstrous lab subject? Pretty damn frustrated. It must be my mind, full of buzzing hormones and boredom, convoluting my boring days with all of that monster smut I read as a teenager.

I stretch out in bed and let out an embarrassed chuckle at myself. But…as shameful as it is, waking up hasn't gotten rid of that throbbing need that the dream awakened in me. I'm a little bit terrified of heading into work horny and having to look the creature who inspired my weird, sexy fantasy in the eye. So, after carefully listening and determining my parents must have already left the house, I dip my hand into my sweatpants for some much-needed self-care, and grind against my own fingers until I find my gasping relief.

Chapter Eleven

Despite my *thorough* attempts to sate the feelings that inspired that dream last night, I still can't shake the memory of it as I sit in the lab later that morning. I chew my lip, drum my pen against the desk, and stare at the Nightmare behind the glass. He—*it*, I tell myself—isn't holding a humanoid form today but remaining a sort of amorphous cloud of darkness, drifting through the cell. But sometimes, as he—*it*—shifts, I swear I catch a glimpse of that humanoid form again.

Doubt creeps in. Maybe I *have* been reading into the subject's behavior. Maybe my mind is mixing up the real Nightmare, who only takes a human form to imitate me, with the made-up figure in my stress dreams.

Dr. Wright warned me to focus on concrete evidence rather than attempts to understand. Maybe this is what she meant. Maybe this is a test of my ability to think rationally. This subject is not human, or close to it. It's just a shadow. A shadow who can nod or shake its head, but that doesn't really *mean* anything. It's not the sort of evidence that will convince anyone, and I shouldn't be letting it convince *me*. If that dream last night proved anything, it's that I'm letting myself sink a little too deep into this. I'm well aware of my tendency to get a little obsessed with things sometimes. I did it when I started investigating the Facility, and I'm doing it again now.

Yet even as I throw myself into my daily tasks, I find my mind drifting. Doubt and suspicion wage a war in the back of my mind no matter how hard I try to focus. If I try to talk to Dr. Wright about this and I'm wrong, it will be humiliating. But if I'm right… If I'm right, then keeping an intelligent being trapped here and running these mind-numbing experiments on it is *cruel*. *I'm* bored of this, and I've only been here for a few days.

And what if they ask me to use that awful Sound 3 and it has a negative reaction again? Even if it possesses nothing more than animal intelligence, I don't think I could bring myself to knowingly hurt the Nightmare. I could always lie and make up notes, but I still don't know exactly how much I'm being observed while working. I've been able to justify my little experiments, but a straight-up lie would definitely get me in trouble.

I groan, leaning back in my chair and brushing my hair out of my face. I stare through the panel at the Nightmare and try to think clearly, without giving in to self-doubt or the lingering, uncomfortable feelings of that weirdly horny dream. I need to think logically about this. I need to think like a scientist running an experiment. This is all a muddled mess, but one thing is clear to me: if I'm going to prove—even to myself— that this thing is really intelligent, then I need to find a way to communicate with the Nightmare. Really communicate in a way that will let it answer with more than *yes* or *no*.

* * *

I spend the rest of the day experimenting with different ways to talk through the glass barrier. I grab my lunch to go—like the mysterious other woman, who I only occasionally encounter for a few seconds at a time before she rushes off—with an apology to Ezra. I scarf it down at my desk as quickly as I can, and then it's back to work.

At first, I try to speak through the intercom or hold up paper with words. The subject's behavior seems to change when I make attempts, growing either agitated or excited, but it doesn't speak back to me in a way I can interpret. It does, however, gradually shift into a more humanoid form. Like it's *trying* to find a shape that will allow it to interact with me more easily. After a couple of hours, I note with amazement that its shape is becoming more solid and more detailed. Facial features emerge from what was once only a blank mask. Soft tendrils like hair float around its head.

And it forms a mouth—a mouth with full lips and a hint of sharp teeth behind them. Prominent cheekbones and long lashes…

More and more like the figure that appeared in my dream.

I blush, remembering how alluring I found the figure then, and still do, if I'm being honest. It also makes me wonder, for one mad moment, if that means the dream was *real*?

But I dismiss it quickly. That's impossible. And yes, this whole situation and the Nightmare's very existence are impossible, but the idea of something infiltrating my dreams is a whole other realm of unreality. Plus, surely, if this subject could enter my dreams, Dr. Wright and the other higher-ups would know. It's not that I have immense trust in Dr. Wright, but…*someone* would've warned me. Right? It'd be dangerous not to. And it would affect my work.

…Unless they don't care. I'm just an expendable employee to them. Or maybe they don't even know what the Nightmare is fully capable of. A chill creeps up my spine as I remember all the conspiracy theories about disappearances in town. They don't seem so ridiculous now that I know they're working with actual monsters here. Maybe some subjects have escaped over the years…or maybe the disappearances have been employees.

But no. Nope. Not gonna let myself get paranoid. There is no *way* this creature can actually affect my dreams. The more logical explanation is that I must've seen the Nightmare form this face before, during one of its other transformations, and my subconscious ran with it in my dream.

I nod to myself, reassured by the logic. The Nightmare mirrors the motion, nodding back, and I suppress a laugh.

"Think you're funny, do you?" I mutter to myself. Humor is another sign of intelligence…but of course, I can't get ahead of myself. I still have no evidence of that. The ability to *mimic* does not equal intelligence. Birds and apes love to imitate human speech and behavior. It's fascinating, but it doesn't *mean* anything. Yet.

I tap my pen against my palm, thinking. "How do I get you to talk…" Writing was a bust, and even now that the subject has formed a mouth, it still isn't speaking, so I have to think of something else to try.

My eyes focus on its long, clawed fingers. They seem close to humanoid, and dexterous, with opposable thumbs. Sign language might be possible. I only have a grasp of the basics of it, but it's a place to start.

After racking my brain to dredge up some of the words I learned in high school, I step up to the glass barrier and carefully move my hands through the motions for *hello, yes, no*, and *please*. I speak the words along with each one. The subject mirrors each one precisely, picking up the motions with surprising speed. It both excites and frightens me to think about how intelligent the being I'm dealing with may be. Even if it's not human-level sentience, if the thing is as smart as a dog or an ape, then it deserves better treatment and far more stimulus than the Facility is giving it.

Once it's mastered the basic words of sign language, I start on the alphabet. I spell my own name out—just M - A - R - A for simplicity—and gesture at myself.

But I can't get the subject to do anything other than imitate me. After several tries, I remember that I still have to finish my instructions for the day and give up for now. I wave goodbye to the subject, resume my seat, and turn the opaqueness on the barrier back up so I can focus on my basic duties.

The Nightmare does not seem pleased about this. It paces back and forth in front of the barrier and refuses to respond to any of the usual stimuli as I run through them. When I press the button for a sound stimulus, its form comes apart—wisps of darkness at its edges going brittle and spiky in a way that feels *angry*—and then, amazingly, it lifts a hand and signs *no*.

I blink. Hit the sound again. Again its hand moves, the gesture angrier this time. *No.*

"It can't be *that* smart," I mutter to myself. "It's just… imitating…"

Still, I can't bring myself to continue with those repetitive instructions. Instead, against my better judgment, I set the envelope aside and hit the button to bring down the barrier again.

The Nightmare straightens.

Yes, it signs at me, and then: *Hello, Mara.*

And its lips pull back to reveal a smile full of sharp, sharp teeth.

87

Chapter Twelve

I'm surprised how easy it is to get Dr. Wright to agree to meet with me. And more surprised that she asks if I'm okay with meeting up outside of work hours. I'm sure she's very busy, and it's true I only had an informal meeting in mind, so I agree… But part of me wonders if there's another motive to this. I know the Facility is decked out in cameras. Is it possible she doesn't want someone there to overhear this? Does she suspect what I'm about to tell her? Is there someone there she doesn't trust?

I don't really trust *her*, if I'm being honest. But she's the best point of contact I have at the Facility. I'm definitely not talking to Ethan about this, and I get the feeling Ezra doesn't have much more power there than I do, so Dr. Wright it is. She invites me for breakfast at her place tomorrow morning. Eight a.m. is hideously early for a Saturday, but that's beside the point right now.

Suddenly, I am unsure of myself. Of the lack of evidence I've gathered. I have nothing but my memory and my words to back me up. Will it be enough?

It has to be. I know I saw what I saw, and that the Nightmare is more intelligent than the people at the Facility seem to understand. Even if she doesn't believe me right away, if I raise the flag on this, it *has* to be enough for Dr. Wright to take a closer look. Hopefully that won't mean taking me off the project... But if it does, I'll have to accept it. This isn't about me. This is about subject X-13. If I'm right, the Nightmare is being grossly mistreated.

And I *am* right. I have to keep believing that. I may not have much in the way of hard evidence, because I can't carry any notes or videos out of the facility, but I know what I've seen and I know that it's gone beyond the boundaries of pure imitation. The subject *is* communicating with me, and it's learning at a rate that implies a high level of intelligence. Now, I just have to find a way to convince Wright.

*　*　*

Of course, after tossing and turning for hours, I fall asleep only to have another damn dream about the Nightmare. I curl up in bed and screw my eyes shut, ignoring the constant, looming presence of the humanoid shadow in the corner.

"Yes, subconscious, I *get* it," I mutter to myself, wishing I could dream about something—anything—else. But this is what I get for obsessing over my upcoming conversation before bed, I guess.

Work is already consuming my days, leaving me exhausted and deprived of human contact... Now, it's following me into my dreams too.

*　*　*

I wake up feeling more tired than ever. God, I was really looking forward to sleeping in on my first weekend since starting the job, but this is important. So I drag myself out of bed and dress professionally in slacks and a silk blouse, slathering the rings under my eyes with makeup.

Still, when I pull up to the address Dr. Wright texted me, I'm quivering a little.

I didn't know houses this nice existed in Ash Valley. It's a beautiful, modern building, all open windows and warm, polished wood, with a perfectly manicured front yard full of pretty succulents and stone steps.

I can't fight the feeling that I'm out of my league, but I made it this far, so I *have* to do this. I take a deep breath, fix my hair in the mirror, and climb the steps to the door.

When Dr. Wright opens it, looking casual in slippers and a pair of relaxed culottes, I feel foolish for dressing up in an attempt to impress her. But she greets me warmly and leads me inside, to a house filled with the warm, yeasty scent of something freshly baked. She gives me a brief tour of a gorgeous living room and state-of-the-art granite kitchen before we settle in the dining room. A beautiful brunch twist on a charcuterie board waits for us, holding a spread of mini bagels with cream cheese and lox, scones with jam and whipped butter, and beautifully arranged pieces of fruit.

"Coffee or tea?" she asks, pouring herself a cup of the latter from a pretty porcelain pot.

"I, um… Tea is fine," I say, since it's already here. Then I immediately curse myself for saying that, because what the hell? I am not a tea person. The cup and plate clatter a little in my hands as I take them, and I clear my throat. "Wow, this is amazing. You didn't have to do all this. Seriously, I usually just grab a bowl of cereal on my way out the door."

She waves a graceful hand. "I like to go all-out on the weekends. I always bake far too many scones. Please, enjoy as much as you'd like."

It's hard to eat when I'm nervous. But the first rich, crumbly mouthful of lemon and blueberry scone helps chase away my nerves. And it's humanizing to watch how thoroughly Dr. Wright enjoys her first bite of one, too, shutting her eyes and humming in unabashed pleasure.

We eat quietly for a few minutes. Once we start to slow down, Dr. Wright wipes her hands on a napkin, sits back, and fixes me with her striking gaze. My mouth goes dry, and I realize, with unfortunate timing, that I am as terrified of this woman as I was the first day she showed up on my doorstep.

"So," she says. "Tell me what's on your mind."

I swallow. The scones suddenly feel heavy as rocks in my stomach, my mouth too dry to speak. I wet it with a mouthful of tea and consider what to say. Dr. Wright strikes me as the sort of person who appreciates getting straight to the point, so that's what I decide on. I clear my throat, fold my hands on my lap, and meet her eyes.

"You told me Subject X-13 isn't intelligent," I say.

She blinks at me across the table. "Yes. Continue."

I pause, mouth open. There were a dozen arguments on the tip of my tongue, but I was expecting her to disagree or challenge me right off the bat, and now I'm losing steam. "I-I… I think you're wrong. I'm pretty sure it's trying to communicate with me."

"Hm." She folds one leg over the other, rests her chin on a palm. "How so?"

"It responds to my voice." Shit. I was—*am*—so sure about

this, but now that I'm given an opportunity to try and prove it, I'm questioning myself. It's making me sound like I have no idea what I'm talking about, even though I *do*.

I wish I had notes, though I know that would be a huge breach of Facility protocol. Having nothing leaves me feeling like I'm grasping at smoke, doubting my own memories. "And it… When I put my hand against the glass, it takes a human shape and does the same." I'm stumbling over my words and can feel color rising to my cheeks as Dr. Wright regards me with an entirely unimpressed expression. I'm getting so flustered that I almost forget my most important piece of evidence. "And—sign language! I'm teaching it sign language. It knows my name."

She sips her tea and regards me over the brim of the cup. The look on her face is almost disappointed, which gives me a strange sinking sensation in my stomach. I didn't come here for her approval, I came ready for an argument, and yet… "Are you certain it's formulating its own sentences and thoughts, rather than imitating yours?"

I bite my lip. I anticipated this question. I *knew* she would probe me to make sure there's no confirmation bias happening, and I wish I had a better answer, or a better reasoning other than my own intuition. "I've only taught it limited words so far. But I feel confident that it's trying to communicate. And it's smart. Really smart. It learns so quickly."

"If good imitation made one intelligent, we would have a very different regard for parrots." She sounds almost bored. Shame crawls up the back of my neck in a slow heat; I feel like I'm trying to lecture an expert on a subject I've just begun to learn. "Is there anything else? Has it spoken aloud? Or communicated in writing?"

"Well, no… But what if it can't? Just because it's intelligent doesn't mean it knows our language or has the same methods of communication that we do. But I… I can feel it, Dr. Wright." I lean forward in my chair. "Maybe if I were able to go into the enclosure with him—it—even for just a couple of minutes—"

"I'm going to stop you there, Mara," she says in such a curt tone that I immediately shut up. I expect her to chew me out, but instead she sighs and shuts her eyes for a moment before continuing with a softer voice. "Look. It's very normal to become attached to one's subject. To begin reading into its behaviors and seeing thoughts and feelings," she says. "I've been through a similar experience."

That snaps me out of wishing I could melt into my chair. "You have?"

"Yes." She clears her throat. For a moment, I'm sure she's about to change the subject, but then a strange look passes over her face and she says, more haltingly than before, "I had…a close encounter with one of the subjects, when I was only a research assistant. I was briefly trapped in the cell with it. And before I could be extracted, I became delusionally certain we had some kind of bond. That there was an intelligent, conscious, *kind* creature locked up in that cell."

"And?" I ask, leaning forward. There's a look I've never seen on her face before. A new, raw emotion caught somewhere between pain and tenderness.

Her expression shutters. Perfectly smooth again. "I learned my lesson when it murdered several lab personnel in a breakout attempt, using me as a hostage."

My chair creaks as I lean back. "Oh."

"Indeed." She taps her long nails on the table and offers a thin, brittle smile. "So trust that I am not relaying empty words when I tell you: what you're experiencing is normal. But you cannot entertain such ideas. These subjects are contained here for a reason. They are not human, or anything akin to human. They are dangerous. And while I do not doubt that they have their own animal intelligence, it is nothing like ours, and it would be a mistake to convince yourself otherwise."

I frown. I hear the logic in what she's saying, and yet… "I don't know anything about the other subjects, but I've had the impression that no two are the same. So how can we assume that each one is similarly unintelligent or dangerous?"

"We make no assumptions at the MRF Center," Dr. Wright says. "There are only facts. I can tell you that your X-13 has been contained here since 1952, and in that time, it has been responsible for the deaths of over a dozen personnel who attempted to connect with it. During its brief escape from confinement in '85, it killed eight people."

That stops me short. Those rumors about disappearances in Ash Valley…they were true after all. Cold fear curls in my chest before settling in my gut. I was warned there'd be risks involved with my work, but it's still shocking to hear that they placed a new employee with something *that* dangerous, even if it's locked in a cell during our interactions. I clear my suddenly dry throat. "How did it kill them?"

She meets my gaze. "Do you really want to know?"

I hesitate. *Want* is a strong word; the sinking feeling in my stomach warns me that I'm not going to like what I'm about to hear if I agree. Yet more than wanting, I think I *need* to hear it—because there's still doubt lingering in my heart. I know I will never fully believe her without some kind of proof. And if that proof exists, then I need to be convinced.

My throat is too tight to speak, but I nod.

I expect her to spin out a grisly tale for me. Instead, she leaves the room and returns with a briefcase. I dimly register that she was prepared for this scenario. Her friendliness, the brunch spread, the casual conversation—they were all a farce. She must have suspected from the moment I contacted her what I was going to say. And she was already prepared to refute me. While I'm still reeling from that, she pulls out a file and slides a series of photographs across the table to me. I reach for them automatically, not really understanding what's happening, but stop as she settles a hand lightly on my wrist.

"These are disturbing," she says, "but I believe it's important for you to see them."

It takes me a moment to understand what is happening. I won't be hearing the evidence from her lips. I'll be seeing it for myself. As she lets go of me, I slowly lower my eyes to the stack of photos and flip the first one over. Bile rises in the back of my throat, but I press a hand to my mouth and keep looking. I look until the image is burned into my eyelids, and then I push it to the side and stare at the next.

I understand now why Dr. Wright chose to give me photographs instead of explaining.

How was my question, and it's not one that's easily answered in words. Even if she had managed to paint the picture, I'm not sure I would have believed it if I didn't see it with my own two eyes.

Most of these pictures are hard to identify as bodies at first glance. They're destroyed brutally, utterly. Torn limb from limb, some with visible teeth marks, others so twisted it's impossible to tell what did the damage. There's a man with gaping black holes where his eyes should be. Another with all ten fingers broken and his ribcage torn out like it burst open from within.

I look at every single photograph in the stack because I feel that I owe it to these people who died so horribly. I have to see. To understand. To avoid repeating their mistakes.

When I look up at Dr. Wright again, tears blur my vision—so I can't tell if my distress has her satisfied, or grim, or anything at all.

But when she speaks, there's no emotion in it. "I trust you understand now why the work we do is necessary and the security measures important."

I nod and sit in numb shock while she retrieves the photographs, places them into her briefcase, and clips it shut in short, brisk movements. "You made the right call in coming to me with these concerns, and I advise that you not bring them up to anyone else." She sets the briefcase aside and looks up at me. "Is there anything else I can do for you?"

I shake my head and mumble some excuse about having to go. She walks me to the door. I still feel numb, distant, like I'm watching this happen from somewhere outside my body. I can't even manage a smile or an appropriate goodbye, but Dr. Wright acts like everything is perfectly fine.

As we reach the door, she stops me with a hand on my arm and squeezes it in a surprisingly gentle motion that breaks through my daze.

"Mara, please don't forget that I personally sought you out as a hire," she says, looking me in the eyes. "It's important to me to build better connections with locals *and* to bring more women into the MRF. I believe you can do good work with us, so please, don't let me down."

Oddly, I have the sense that she means it. If she didn't, it would probably be easy for her to dismiss me from my job right now. *Unsuited to a high-stress work environment*, I think distantly, remembering Ethan's words. That helps me pull myself together, and I manage a weak smile and a small nod.

"I understand," I say. "Thank you for the advice, Dr. Wright."

"My pleasure," she says.

Still, as the door shuts behind me, I'm left feeling utterly alone.

Chapter Thirteen

Sunday passes by too quickly. I finally get a chance to sleep in, and I take full advantage of it, dozing until well into the afternoon. Even when I manage to pull myself out of bed, I luxuriate in my freedom to do nothing. When my parents get back from their weekend hike, I'm on the couch in my pajamas, eating a bag of chips and binging true crime documentaries.

"Oh, hi, honey," my mom says, hovering in the doorway while my dad heads into the kitchen to start making dinner. "No big plans this weekend? New work friends?" She eyes me in a way that is probably meant as worried but feels judgmental.

"Um…" I swallow a thick mouthful of chips and self-consciously wipe my greasy hands on my sweatpants. "I had brunch with a new work friend yesterday, actually."

Friend is a very strong word for Dr. Wright, and I feel a twinge of guilt for lying, but the way my mom's concern dissipates is worth it.

"Oh, that's great," she says, beaming at me. "I'm so glad you're settling back into town."

I force myself to smile back and agree to eat dinner with her and my dad, even as uncertainty grows like a weight in my gut.

I don't want her to be concerned, but honestly, now that I'm thinking about it, *I'm* a little concerned about myself. I've been self-isolating, obsessing over work…acting almost as crazy as Ethan once accused me of being. Self-doubt creeps in and makes a home in the back of my mind, but I do my best to push it down. At least Dr. Wright shut down my delusions before they could go any further. And I *will* do better this week. I'll be normal. I will not screw up the only goddamn opportunity that life has handed me.

* * *

I expect myself to feel frightened when I sink into my observation chair Monday morning. Instead, I just feel… numb. Disappointed, almost. Whether it's because I was so wrong about the subject, or because I let myself be fooled so thoroughly by what's apparently a vicious monster, I'm not sure. Either way, I know that neither Dr. Wright nor the subject are to blame. This is all on me.

I got carried away by my imagination and probably my ego, too, thinking I had discovered something new about the subject that they've been studying here for decades. I should be grateful that Dr. Wright had the good sense—and the evidence—to drag me back to planet Earth before I got myself killed.

When I think about those photographs again, I shudder and squeeze my eyes shut in an attempt to blot them out. But it's good that I saw them. They were convincing in a way that even Dr. Wright's best logic couldn't be. Now I know that I need to keep my distance from this subject, no matter what my romantic, self-indulgent side says.

"Back to our regularly appointed schedule," I mutter, and retrieve today's set of instructions from the envelope on the desk. Just checking responses to various stimuli on the control panel again. Regular, boring…safe.

Still, as I open the observation window and find the Nightmare waiting for me in its human shape, head cocked to one side and something like anticipation in its stature, I feel a flicker of sadness. But I squash it as ruthlessly as I can and start to carry out my instructions.

* * *

If I hadn't had Dr. Wright so firmly deny my suspicions, I would be reading into the Nightmare's behavior this week. Surely I'm just letting my imagination get the better of me, but it's hard to look at the way it's acting and describe it in a way other than *frustrated*. Or *angry*, maybe. Before I started veering away from my instructions, it responded to the various stimuli in a fairly predictable pattern. Now that I return to the routine and stop adding my own tests, it's behaving completely differently. Sometimes it sulks in a corner and refuses to respond at all; other times, it flings itself at the observation window, throwing gnashing teeth and writhing tentacles and pounding fists against the glass. Once, it even throws its chair, making me flinch, though it only bounces away harmlessly, the barrier absorbing the impact with a tiny *thump* to show for it.

But I am trying to be objective here. So I don't use words like *sullen* or *angry* or *betrayed* to describe its behavior, even when my brain whispers them, and my stomach churns with guilt, and my hand shakes as I write my notes. I record everything with as little bias as I can and continue with my instructions the way I'm supposed to.

I'm surprised how emotionally exhausting it is. The first week was so exciting, each day feeling like a new breakthrough or discovery. Returning to this dull routine and rote instruction feels soul-sucking. Like admitting defeat. No matter how curious I am about certain aspects of the job, I'm not sure how long I can keep this up if things continue like this.

Especially when every night, I fall asleep and dream of the Nightmare glaring at me from the corner, his eyes full of accusation.

* * *

I spend all week grinding through tasks, chatting with Ezra at lunch, and thinking about the upcoming weekend. Yet when it arrives, I find myself at a loss. Work keeps me so busy that I barely have time to think about anything else. But over the weekend, I'm left with far too many vacant hours, and I don't want my mom sliding back into worry mode. I should start looking into my own place, now that I have a steady income, but I keep procrastinating—still unsure if I *really* want to build a life for myself here in Ash Valley. Every step toward settling myself here feels like a step away from ever escaping.

So for now, I'm still stuck at my childhood home. My parents are surprisingly busy with the routine they've settled into in my absence. My dad goes to a sports bar to watch games with his friends, my mom has a hiking group and a book club at the library, and they also have a weekly date night at Cheesecake Factory. It's adorable, and it makes me feel even more like a sad sack for sitting at home alone. Not sad enough to accept the half-hearted invitation to third wheel their cheesecake date, though. I wave them off with a lie that I have plans to meet a new work friend out tonight and tell them not to wait up for me.

As the door shuts behind them, I slump back against the couch. Why did I say that? Now they'll be even more concerned if they come back and I'm still here. Maybe even unpleasantly surprised if they're expecting some post-date-night—urgh—"quality time." I shudder at the thought, grab my phone, and hastily scroll through my options for getting out of this goddamn house.

There aren't many. But there is one local bar with half-decent reviews. *The Dustpan* is not a promising name, but I can't afford to be choosy. Plus, I remember seeing the place as a teenager and being curious about what it might be like inside, after catching a tantalizing glimpse of neon lights and pool tables. The last time I was in Ash Valley, I was still too young to be allowed past the door. So I might as well check it out.

If only I had some company to enjoy it with. I'd text Ezra, but I don't have any way to contact him outside of work. A scroll through my contact list leaves me feeling progressively more despondent. Everyone I want to hang out with is back in California. I shoot off an *I miss you* text to Amy and try hitting up an old high school friend on Instagram, but it turns out she's busy with her two young children at home. Shows how much I've been keeping up with things back here. I catch up with her and send lots of heart eye emojis in response to pics of her incredibly adorable toddlers. It leaves me feeling a little less isolated, but I still have no one to go out with.

But screw it. Alone or not, I enjoy having an excuse to look nice. I take my time showering, doing my hair, and giving myself a simple cat-eye and red lip. Then I pull out a little black dress and snakeskin heels I haven't had an excuse to wear since I was in the city. I might be a little overdressed for a small-town dive bar, but whatever. I'll accept the curse of being the hottest bitch in the Dustpan if I must.

* * *

When I pull up in the back of an Uber, the amount of beat-up pickup trucks in the parking lot is almost enough to make me change my mind. But then I think of spending the night eating ice cream alone and waiting for my parents to get back from their date and force myself to get out and march up to the door. I'm almost disappointed there's no one to check my ID after all of those teenage fantasies about sneaking in, but my first whiff of booze chases that disappointment away.

The music might be a little hokey and the floor a bit sticky, and the whole place smells like cigarette smoke and stale beer, but it still feels good to be out at a bar. It's also a much-needed ego boost to catch heads turning my way. And the place is surprisingly lively, even though most of the patrons are either twice my age or look uncomfortably like people I half remember from high school. I *really* do not want to end up in a long conversation about memories and poorly disguised jabs about my missed potential…but maybe after a couple drinks I'll be able to stomach it more easily. I head over to the bar, hop onto a rickety stool, and order a beer.

The bartender is a woman about ten years my senior and *very* attractive, with long, dark hair and a sleeve of faded tattoos. I'm tempted to flirt with her—I *have* been awfully lonely, and she's the only person here I'd even consider going home with— but it seems like she has enough on her hands. The other, drunker, overwhelmingly male patrons are already leering at her low-cut top and trying to drag her into conversations. So I keep it polite, though the wink she gives me along with my beer makes me note I might want to try on another, quieter night.

I sip my beer and look around, drinking in the atmosphere along with the alcohol. After the monotony of work and living with my parents, it feels pretty good to be somewhere new and reasonably interesting. I watch a group of men with the same bad haircut argue over a pool game, and a highly intoxicated couple dancing progressively more inappropriately on the almost-empty dance floor.

As trashy as the last sight is, I can't stop glancing over, and I'm ashamed to find that it sparks a hint of longing in me. God, it's been a long time since I've been laid. But aside from the overworked and much-harassed bartender, there isn't anyone I would dream of fucking in this place. I grimace down at my drink and wonder if I should call it an early night and retire with my vibrator and a spicy book for company.

When I feel a tap on my shoulder, I expect it's a fifty-fifty between finding an old high school friend or being hit on by someone wearing cowboy boots—but instead, I turn and find myself looking up at Ethan.

My mouth drops open. "Oh, hey!"

"Hey yourself." He smiles. "Surprised to see you here.

Doesn't seem like your vibe." He looks good, in a tight V-neck and dark jeans. It's annoying. Especially when I glance past him and see the young blonde he's here with, while I'm alone at the bar.

I smile, hoping it doesn't look as fake as it feels. "Not a lot of places to be in this town."

He laughs. "Fair enough." Then, catching me glancing at her again, he steps aside and gestures to his companion. "Oh, right! This is Belle. She also works at—" He catches himself, glancing around, and adds in a lower voice, "Well, you know." He winks—actually winks, ew, he really cannot pull it off like the hot bartender can—and adds to Belle, "I sort of helped get Mara set up there."

Fucker. He most certainly did not. But I decide to let that pass, and instead offer a more genuine grin to Belle than the one I gave Ethan. "Hey, I'm Mara." When I get a closer look, I realize, with a shock, that I recognize her. This is the other female employee that I share my lunch with, the one who is always rushing off without talking to anyone. It's odd that she's here with Ethan, since she always seems to pointedly ignore him…but maybe what I mistook for dislike was actually her attempt to keep her work and personal life separate.

I study her as she shakes my hand with a small, shy smile that I can't help but find endearing. She's way too pretty to hang out with a guy like Ethan. "I've seen you around, but I don't think we've ever been introduced. What do you do there?"

"Research assistant," she says, so quietly, I barely hear her above the music.

"Oh, me too!" I'm dying of curiosity wondering what kind of subject she ended up with, but I know that we've both signed an extensive NDA preventing either of us from talking about it. In fact, I'm not sure if we can really say anything about the job other than what's already been said, so the conversation quickly tapers into awkward silence.

"Well, cheers to nondisclosure agreements," I say, raising my glass, and she laughs and loosens up a bit.

After slurping down the rest of my drink and then a second, I decide it's best to get straight to the point the next time Ethan heads off to the bathroom. I lean in. "So, are you and Ethan…you know…?"

She flushes bright red. "Oh, no. No, no. He's my manager."

I quirk a brow. "Yet you're out drinking with him?"

She turns an even deeper red, though I didn't think it was possible. "He was…persistent. And kind of implied it wasn't just going to be the two of us out tonight." She tucks a strand of loose hair behind her ear and drops her eyes. "But that was probably my mistake."

I barely know this woman, but still I feel indignant anger on her behalf. That sounds like Ethan. So damn slippery, he makes you doubt your own memory. I want to warn her about him, but just as I open my mouth, I spot him winding through the crowd back toward us. So instead I scoot closer to Belle and loop my arm through hers. "Well, I'm not going anywhere," I tell her, and she gives me a relieved smile.

I stop drinking after that, just so I can keep a close eye on everything between the two of them. Every time Ethan tries to engage Belle in a too-personal conversation or lead her away for any reason, I lean into my white-girl-wastedness and loudly insert myself between them. I can tell Ethan is getting frustrated behind that pasted-on smile, but he's too busy playing the Nice Guy to actually call me out for "cockblocking" him, as he no doubt thinks I'm doing. Belle feigns concern for my well-being and reluctance to leave my side because of it, while shooting me grateful looks and sly little smiles whenever Ethan's not looking.

This is not how I pictured my night going, but I don't regret it. By the time the bar starts emptying, I feel like I've made a new friend in Belle—and a fresh enemy in Ethan, but that's okay. I'm sure he was always out to get me anyway. And though it's possible it's going to affect my job, that's not more important to me than making sure poor Belle doesn't make the same mistakes that I did.

As we head out for the night, Belle insists that Ethan gives me a ride home instead of letting me take an Uber by myself. I'm ready to drag her into my parents' house if I have to, but thankfully her house is closer to the bar than mine. I insist we drop her off first—though she seems worried, and gives me her phone number "just in case," I'm certain I can handle this.

Unfortunately, that also means I'm alone with a pissed-off Ethan afterward. I fiddle with my phone and stare out the window, pretending not to notice his frosty silence creating a growing tension in the car.

"It's sad to see you like this, Mara," he says eventually.

I roll my eyes at the window. Even though I badly want to retort, I just don't care enough to get myself embroiled in an argument right now. "Uh-huh."

"I'm serious. You always seemed like you had so much ahead of you, and now…here you are. You wouldn't even have your job at the Facility if not for me." I grind my teeth, resisting the urge to retort. Even if he *did* put in a good word for me—which I highly doubt—that doesn't mean he deserves all the credit. But he's always been good at convincing himself of his own narrative. "You're too smart to be acting like this."

"And you're too sleazy to be hitting on girls like Belle," I say before I can stop myself. I'm aware it would be better to keep my mouth shut, but he knows just how to hit my buttons.

He sighs like he's disappointed. "Is that what this is about? Are you jealous?"

"God, no." I suppress the urge to bang my head against the window. How long can this car ride take?

"Are you sure? Because you've certainly been going out of your way to spend time with me since you got back here. First you invite me out for coffee, then you get a job at the same place I'm working, now you mysteriously show up at the bar I go to every weekend—"

"I am the *opposite* of interested, Ethan," I snap at him. "You lied to me. You gaslighted me and cheated on me. You made me feel like I was fucking crazy."

He sighs again—the patient, world-weary sigh of a parent dealing with a misbehaving child. "Whatever you want to tell yourself, Mara," he says, as though he's taking the high ground. "I'm not going to argue anymore. You're not capable of having a rational conversation when you're like this."

With that one line, it feels like I'm a confused, angry teenager again, left wondering if I really am the one with the problem. It makes me want to scream. It makes me want to claw his eyes out. For a blissful moment, I let myself picture it: going absolutely feral on him, ripping him apart with nails and teeth. It feels fucking *good*.

But instead of doing that, I shut my eyes and force myself into silence for the remainder of the drive home. As soon as the vehicle comes to a stop, I fling the door open and march away before I can say anything more that I'll regret in the morning.

He's not worth my time.

Chapter Fourteen

I try to be as quiet as possible as I stumble to my room, since it's clearly way past my parents' bedtime, but my body doesn't seem to be on the same page as my mind. I stumble and stub my toe, trip into the wall, and knock my toiletries off the counter multiple times while going through my bedtime routine. I'm not even *that* drunk—my buzz has long since plateaued and started to fade—but I'm tired and cranky after that conversation with Ethan. Fucking Ethan and his fucking high horse. I could've had a good time tonight, maybe even gotten laid, but instead I had to save that poor girl from him and suffer through the car ride home.

It's exhausting, carrying all of this impotent anger inside of me. By the time I finally crawl into bed, I'm too tired to pull out the vibrator I've been thinking about all night.

* * *

When I open my eyes, he's here again, standing over the bed. My Nightmare. I'm not scared now, nor even surprised. Though I am a *little* disappointed, because I was hoping I could escape Ash Valley in my dreams, at least. Maybe have a nice spicy fantasy. I feel like I have spent so much time bottling myself up—my shame and my anger and my desire—that I feel like I'm about to burst, even in my sleep.

"Am I going to dream about you forever?" I ask, tilting my head to look at the Nightmare at the foot of the bed.

"Is there something else you'd rather dream of?" I haven't heard that low, delicious voice in a while, and I can't ignore the effect on me. I bite the inside of my cheek as he drifts closer, huge, spindly hands gripping the end of my bed frame. The tips of his claws scratch over the wood. I eye them, wondering. Such big hands. I bet he could grab me around the waist and lift me with only one.

The thought should frighten me, but it does quite the opposite.

"If I did, would you leave?" I ask, not because I want him to, but because I'm curious.

"No." His form doesn't move so much as it stretches, like a shadow lengthening with the passage of the sun, and all of a sudden he's closer. Sitting on the edge of my bed. That familiar scent hits me again: smoke and spice, like campfire and black pepper. I used to associate it with fear, but now it makes my mouth water. "But I can be whatever you want me to be." His form goes hazy and indistinct, becoming the cloud of darkness I usually see within the cell when I work. Various shapes and faces swim out of the darkness. I recognize a raven's wing, a snake's tongue, a weeping woman who looks disturbingly like me, Ethan with his look of stern disapproval.

I flinch at the last one. "No," I say. I sit up slowly. Normally, I hold up the blankets to cover my scanty nightclothes—it is so damn hot in this room at night, I always go to bed wearing relatively little—but this time I don't. Even as the covers pool on my lap, revealing pale slivers of bare thigh beneath the T-shirt and panties I'm wearing.

The Nightmare gradually shifts back into his usual humanoid form. He's even closer than before. Nearly close enough to touch. "No?" he asks. "Tell me what you want."

This is just a dream, right? And my dreams are mine to mold as I will. In my real life, I am trapped in this town, in my job, in my parents' house. But here? Here, no one can shame me for who I am or what I want. No one can judge me for what I do.

I push the covers away and sit forward, resting on my knees in the middle of the bed. Then I reach out, slowly, and touch the Nightmare's cheek. I trace a finger over the hard line of his jaw, his full lower lip. "I like this face," I whisper. "Sharp teeth and all."

He goes still under my touch, his eyes on me. "You are a strange human," he murmurs, his voice lower and raspier than before.

"You're a strange nightmare," I counter, scooting closer, growing bolder. My oversized T-shirt slips off one shoulder, and his eyes follow the motion.

He reaches out to cup my face with one huge hand; even with claws, he is gentle. So gentle, his long fingers warm and velvety against my skin. I shut my eyes and sigh as his finger drifts over my bottom lip. I open my mouth and take it in, sucking gently. When I look up at him, his head is tilted and still, his own mouth open to reveal a glimpse of those sharp, sharp teeth. I am surprised at how well his shadowy features can convey surprise and *desire*.

His form flickers, nearly losing its shape. I pull away from his finger, uncertain and suddenly shy, and shadowy tendrils curl around my wrists, my ankles, my neck. He pins me to the bed beneath his massive form. Rather than trapped or afraid, I feel cradled, *caressed*. This isn't a threat. It's the embodiment of all the dark desires I've never spoken aloud. The fantasies I never trusted anyone enough to play out in real life. Ethan and other guys like him always shamed me for my tastes, my insatiable hunger, and they didn't even know the half of it.

"Brave little Mara," he says. The shadowy tendrils tighten around my limbs and lift me up, so I'm dangling a couple inches above the bed with my wrists above my head. I wriggle in my bindings, but there's no use; his grip is soft but firm, impossible to escape. Meanwhile, his humanoid body sits on the bed and gazes up at me with an aloofness that shouldn't stoke the flames higher. "You think that you could handle me?"

Even as my heart thumps in my ears, I grin down at him. "I'd certainly like to try," I murmur.

And I mean it. I am too fucking curious for my own good.

In a flash, he has me pinned to the bed beneath him again, sharp teeth snapping inches from my face.

"Are you trying to scare me?" I ask, still grinning. Feeling reckless and wild and dangerous. Here, I am free and in control. "I thought we were past this." I try to lift my hips to press against him, seeking much-needed friction, but I can barely move. Still, I manage to lean forward just enough to kiss him. I press my lips to the side of his mouth, and then again—carefully, holding my breath—to one of those huge, sharp canines. He stares down at me, unmoving, but there's a flicker of hunger in his eyes. "Give me what I want," I whisper, holding his gaze. "This is *my* dream."

He huffs a laugh. "If you say so."

He trails one claw down the front of my shirt. I wish he would tear it, but he doesn't. He makes me wait as I squirm and whimper. Then the tip of his claw reaches my panties, and he stops.

"Oh, come on," I say.

He grins. "Say please."

I glare at him, indignant. "You think—" I start, and then a shadowy tendril wraps around my throat, applying a delicious pressure, and I choke off in a breathy moan. *"Please,"* I gasp.

The dark chuckle of his response echoes around the room. Another shadowy tendril yanks my panties down, and then he's on top of me, pressing me down into the bed. He bites my shoulder as he thrusts into me, and the pain mingled with pleasure is so intense, it renders me incoherent. I gasp and whimper as his sharp teeth dig into my shoulder and he sinks deeper into me. He's so big. Too big, especially with hardly any foreplay. The pressure makes my eyes water. It feels like I'm going to be ripped in half, yet I rock my hips against him, eager for more, *more.* This roughness is exactly what I'm craving, exactly what I need to satisfy the hunger and frustration I've been bottling up for weeks. Just when I think I can't possibly handle it, he's fully in and no longer too big, but just big enough to fill me entirely, a perfect fit.

Because of course he is, I think, as his shadowy form shivers around the edges. He can change at will, and right now he is using that to give me my every dark desire. I'm panting as he pulls back, and then he slams into me again, and pleasure chases away every thought.

It's like he knows exactly what I want, what I need, pushing me to my limits without ever stepping past them. He fucks me slowly even as I beg for more, deep thrusts that fill me until my eyes roll back and I'm making desperate, needy sounds. A dozen shadowy hands tease me, pulling my hair, caressing my breasts, pushing into my mouth to force it open when I try to swallow my cries. Fingers become tentacles become a slide of his long tongue, a constantly shifting array of pleasure, teasing and torturing every inch of me. Tears leak from the corners of my eyes and my breath rasps in my throat and God, I need more; it feels like I will never have enough.

It would be humiliating, to be reduced to such a begging, incoherent mess by a real man; I would be self-conscious about my whimpering pleas and the faces I'm making, the way my body arches and contorts, the filthy, wet sounds of my body and the desperation in the things I'm asking him to do to me. But this is just a dream, just my own fantasy, and so there is nothing to hold me back from taking my pleasure as I want it.

So I do. I pour out my every desire, needy and greedy and desperate though it may be. I ask him to choke me and bite me and use me as he will, and he obliges, till I am putty under his many shadowy hands and his long tongue, and the pleasure is so intense I can hardly take it. His rasping breath in my ear, the slide of his tongue against the side of my neck and the bright flares of pain of his teeth, his low moans of pleasure—it all only heightens my own need. But the slow rhythm of his movements stay painfully controlled, keeping me on the edge but never allowing me to reach my peak. Finally, I am reduced to only a single coherent word, a repeated plea: *please, please, please.*

Breath hisses through his teeth as he increases his thrusting, as the wave of pressure inside me builds and builds and builds and then crashes. I cry out as I come, toes curling and body trembling. He fucks me through the orgasm, hard and relentless thrusts, until he groans and shudders too.

He leaves an empty ache when he pulls out of me: a pleasant, satisfying throb between my legs. Slowly, the shadowy tendrils release my ankles and wrists, one by one. I am too tired to lift my head or open my eyes. When I finally manage to crack an eyelid, he is gone, morning light is spilling through my window, and I am awake.

Chapter Fifteen

y sheets are a tangled mess, my pillow is on the floor, and I'm sprawled spread-eagle with my nightshirt pushed up around my waist.

Holy. Shit. I sit up slowly, groaning as I find my body sore and aching, as though I really did get railed by a seven-foot-tall shadow monster last night. Was I thrashing around in my sleep?

Was the dream really *that* good?

Honestly, yes, it was. Still, this is embarrassing. A true testament to the hell of a dry spell I'm going through right now. I drag myself out of bed with a groan and look in the mirror.

Oh. My. God. With my smeared eyeliner, bird's nest hair, and rumpled shirt hanging off one shoulder, I really look like I *actually* had a wild night, rather than just dreaming one up. I snort out a laugh and then sneak to the bathroom for a quick shower before my parents can see me and get the wrong idea. As I scrub my skin, I swear I catch a whiff of smoke and pepper.

I would've thought that having a sex dream would leave me hornier than ever, but instead, I feel sated. I almost Google "is it possible to have orgasms in your sleep," but then decide I'd rather not research what seems like a great thing. Talk about no strings attached.

Still, I do feel a little embarrassed. Sure, it's just a dream, and I know I can't control my brain, but that was a *bizarre* one. I'm pretty sure most women's scandalous sex dreams involve exes or forbidden romances, not shadow monsters from a lab they work in.

But eh, I can't complain. Except for the fact that my dream hookup was undoubtedly the best sex I've ever had, and my imaginary monster a much more generous and exciting lover than any I've had in real life, and *that* is pathetic.

* * *

I should be hungover today, but I'm not. Not even the memory of Ethan's snide lecture can dampen my mood. I'm feeling good enough to drive over to Cup o' Happy, grab myself an iced maple butter latte and a deliciously flaky cheese-and-raspberry pastry, and eat at a table outside in the Sunday sunshine.

At some point, I'm going to have to confront the fact that I had a strange, amazing, and definitely inappropriate sex dream about the monster I work with, and I know it. Walking into the lab tomorrow is going to be awkward. But for now, I'm just going to bask in the afterglow. At least, that's my plan before my phone buzzes in my pocket.

I'm surprised to see an email from work on a Sunday afternoon. But that surprise is soon overshadowed by dread as I skim the brief contents: *Come directly to Room 105 instead of normal post tomorrow. Important matter to discuss. - Dr. Wright.*

Not even a polite salutation or a sign-off. What a power

move. Does she write all of her emails like that, or is it *meant* to come off as cold and intimidating? I let out a nervous laugh and put my phone into my pocket again as if hoping it will let me forget. But it's too late—the pastry's gone to ashes in my mouth, and the day is ruined. I know that Dr. Wright can be curt, but God, that email was something else. She *must* know that leaving so much open to interpretation means I'm going to assume the worst, right? It's impossible to ignore the feeling like I'm being called into the principal's office. I've barely seen her since our embarrassing run-in last weekend, and I've been behaving myself this week.

What did I do to earn such ire from Dr. Wright? Or maybe it's bigger than her. Am I getting fired? Have I done something wrong? This could be about the unauthorized experiments I was running for a while, but it seems odd to confront me a week after I *stopped* doing them. I run frantically through my memories of the last week, trying to figure out if I broke protocol despite my best attempts to do things right. Did I forget to turn in my notes at the end of the day? I don't *remember* doing anything wrong, but I've been so sleep deprived and racked by confusing feelings. It's possible I was on autopilot and did something stupid.

And if I do get fired, what does that mean for me? I wasn't even sure I wanted to stay there long term, but now that I'm thinking about it, my job at the Facility doesn't feel like the sort of thing that's easy to walk away from.

I know I'm getting myself all worked up over very little, but I can't fight the cold sweat that breaks out across my body, imagining terrifying scenarios of being sued for violation of my NDA, or faced with a military tribunal, or a *treason* charge, or, or, or...

Or they know about my dreams. And thus my completely inappropriate feelings for the monster I'm studying.

No, no. It's a distinct possibility that the Facility is tracking everything I do and say to protect their secrecy, but there's no way they're also tracking what I *think*. Still, I imagine sitting across from Dr. Wright and listening to her say I'm fired for my weird horny dreams, and want to die of embarrassment. It's hard to shake the thought once it occurs. No matter how ludicrous it is, the timing is suspicious…

But considering that makes me think of another far more likely scenario. Yesterday was also the day I fought with Ethan. Could this have something to do with him? Is he undermining me? Trying to get me fired? Did I make some HR violation?

The thought of it plagues me with anxiety for the entire ride home. I push away the concerns about my dream to worry about more plausible and equally—well, almost equally—embarrassing and unfortunate scenarios. They can't fire me for dreaming, but I'm sure there are plenty of other reasons that would leave me jobless, stranded, and embarrassed. And possibly followed by FBI agents for the rest of my life. Or the CIA. Which one would this fall under? I consider Googling it, but then remember the Facility may be tracking my internet activity and start sweating anew.

Instead, I pace in my room and run through things that I could've done wrong. The rest of the day passes in a haze, my good mood vanquished, as I try and fail not to spiral into ever-darker depths.

Most of these scenarios are unlikely, I'll admit, born from anxiety rather than logic. Then again, this whole job has been unlikely. I had no idea what to expect when I walked in, but I certainly wasn't prepared for what I was going to find. At this point, nothing feels impossible.

After an evening of stress-binging Netflix and a sad dinner of microwaved pizza in bed, I fall into a fitful sleep. There's no reprieve there. I find myself dreaming of my bedroom again, constantly aware of the morning creeping closer. The Nightmare is here again, but I do my best to ignore him. This time he only sits in the corner and watches me, as though he can sense my mood.

Chapter Sixteen

I don't feel rested in the morning. However, it's time to face my reckoning. I bury my exhaustion under makeup—doing my eyeliner twice because my hand won't stop shaking—and throw on a particularly professional outfit before heading to the Facility.

I swear I can feel eyes on me as I walk through security and down the long hallway toward the room where I'm supposed to meet Dr. Wright. But it's empty except for me, making my heels echo eerily. It feels strange to pass by my usual lab and head deeper into the building, like I'm trespassing somewhere I'm not supposed to be. But soon I find the room and pause outside to wipe my sweaty palms on my pants and straighten my shirt.

When I step into the room, panic hits like a fist to the gut. I wasn't sure what to expect when I walked in here, but it certainly wasn't to see Ethan, Dr. Wright, and an older man I don't recognize sitting on one side of a table, and an empty chair on the other. It looks like a job interview, or an intervention, or... God, I don't know, but definitely something awful.

"Have a seat," Ethan says, flashing his usual amiable grin. But

I don't relax; I know not to trust that smile. I stay wary as I lower myself into the chair. It's hard metal, uncomfortable, and shorter than the seats the others are in, so that I feel small and vulnerable beneath them.

But it's been designed for that, I tell myself. It's meant to make me feel tiny and weak, urge me to confess my wrongdoings or accept abuse from my superiors, and I'm not going to do either. I stiffen my spine even as metal digs into it and plaster on a smile. "Good morning," I say. "What is this about?"

"Oh, nothing bad," Ethan says, again in a carefully warm voice. I don't trust it for one second.

I glance at Dr. Wright for more insight, and she gives me the tiniest nod. It's oddly reassuring, making me think of her words to me the last time we met, about how she wants me to keep working here. But the man I don't recognized is tight-lipped and stony-faced. He looks to be somewhere in his fifties, with a close-cropped beard and hair that might be called salt-and-pepper by someone generous, though there's very little pepper left. Wire-framed glasses frame a pair of intense blue eyes under bushy brows, a combined image that could make him look like a genial grandfather but somehow don't. Instead, he looks more like a retired military man, or the kind of politician who opposes basic human rights for women. I dislike him on sight, and the way he looks at me—somewhere between contemptuous and bored—does not warm me to him.

"We'd like to ask you a few questions about your experiences with Subject X-13." I'm relieved when Dr. Wright speaks up. I don't trust her much, but she still feels like the closest thing to an ally I have in this room.

I clasp my hands in my lap. "Of course. Though I'm not sure

how much insight I can provide, given that I record all of my observations as per the facility guidelines."

Dr. Wright's lips lift in a *very* slight smile.

"And we're very pleased with your notes," Ethan says, dripping with fake sweetness. "Our questions pertain to your experiences outside of the Facility."

My brow furrows. I stare at him, perplexed. "I don't have any experiences with the subject outside of the Facility," I say slowly.

"None at all?" Ethan asks.

"Am I being…accused of something? Because I don't—"

"We're talking about dreams." Now, for the first time, the older man speaks up. His voice is a gruff bark that makes me feel like I'm being told off, even though his words aren't explicitly aggressive. "Are you dreaming about the subject?"

It's such a strange question that I'm not sure how to respond. I look at Dr. Wright, who gives me another tiny, encouraging nod.

"Well?" the man prompts, impatient.

"I… I mean, yes," I admit, flustered. It feels like a strangely private question, even though I'm certain there's no way they can know about the content of these dreams. I can feel my cheeks growing hot, and I'm sure one of them is going to suspect, and oh *God* I need to start thinking about something else right now before I get even more flustered and give myself away. "Sorry, I'm not quite sure how this is relevant to my work." I pause, and after recovering some of my courage, add, "Nor do I believe what I dream about in my free time is any business of my employer."

The man's eyebrows draw together and his lips dip in a displeased scowl. I brace myself, but it's Dr. Wright who speaks.

"You are, of course, under no obligation to disclose anything you do not wish to, and I am sure Director Ramsey did not mean to imply anything to the contrary," she says, but with a pointed look at the man beside her. *Director Ramsey*; I commit the name and important title to memory. I remember Ezra mentioning that Ethan is his protégé of sorts, and another piece of the puzzle slides into place. "But it may be important evidence as to the nature of the subject."

I will myself to end this here, to tell them I don't feel comfortable disclosing anything and walk out—but I'm too curious. She's snagged my attention with that last bit of information, dangled like a worm on a hook, as I'm sure she's planned to. "How so?"

"I'm afraid we would need to hear the content of any dreams you're willing to share before we tell you more. Otherwise, there is a risk of the information contaminating your recollections."

I gnaw on my bottom lip, considering that. It's frustrating, it's surely bait…but it does make sense when I think about it. If I assume they're asking because it's part of the nature of the subject…and that means that others before me have dreamed of the Nightmare…of course they would want to collect that data. But if they reveal too much, it would be impossible to tell if I was only saying what I think they want to hear.

I sigh, my shoulders slumping, and all three of the people on the other side of the table perk up noticeably as they wait to hear my response.

"I dream about it every night," I admit. *It,* not *him,* because I don't want them to catch on to how I've started to think about the subject. "I thought it was just work bleeding into my mind at night."

"When did the first dream occur?" Dr. Wright asks. Dr. Ramsey gives her a meaningful look, and after a moment, she lets out a small sigh and grabs a pen and clipboard from the table in front of her.

I think back. "Well...the night after my first day here, I dreamed that *I* was the one locked inside the cell and being observed. But it was the next night when I started to dream that the Nightmare was visiting me in my bedroom." The night after I brought down the privacy screen and he saw my face for the first time, I remember in a moment of uneasiness.

They question me for hours. I'm asked to describe my dreams in excruciating detail, sometimes multiple times, while Dr. Wright takes detailed notes and the men occasionally murmur to each other in a way that makes me want to stab something. But I don't. I force myself to be patient, taking my notes from Dr. Wright's obsequiousness. It isn't lost on me that she is clearly more highly qualified and experienced than Ethan, but is still the one stuck taking notes; I don't have to question why. Everything about this Director Ramsey guy screams *old school* in the worst kind of way, and his silent judgment speaks to a position of power.

So I answer the questions. Most of them, at least. I don't admit to the content of some of those dreams. The...intimate ones. I don't think I could force myself to describe *those* dreams even if one of them were holding a gun to my head. Sometimes, Dr. Wright's scrutiny makes me feel like she suspects I'm holding back, perhaps even has an inkling of *what* I'm holding back. But before I can squirm too much, she always returns to her notetaking without questioning me. Nor does anyone lift an eyebrow the few times I slip up and call the Nightmare *him* instead of *it*.

Finally, I sink down in my chair, drained. I've recounted everything that I'm willing to disclose: the apparition I've seen in dreams of my bedroom, the way he first frightened me but eventually started having normal conversations, and how curious he seemed about me. Now my own curiosity is burning.

"I take it I'm not the first one this has happened to," I say when the questions finally stop coming. The two men are engaged in a quiet conversation behind their hands again, but Dr. Wright turns her full attention to me.

"No," she says, setting her pen aside and folding her hands in front of her. "Anyone who has worked closely with Subject X-13 has experienced the dreams. We did not warn you, just like we did not warn any of them, because we did not want to risk contaminating the data with expectations. But as it stands, anyone who has observed the subject has dreamed of it the following night, and every night they spend in close proximity."

"So I wasn't here to conduct experiments. I was here to be a part of one." Anger rises within me, but as they only give me indifferent looks in response, that fire drowns under a wave of anxiety. They don't care, and there's nothing I can do about it. I shut my eyes for a moment, sick at how absolutely helpless I feel. As much as I want to continue being angry, I guess I have to focus on being practical instead. "Does…does this mean I'm going to dream about it forever?" My voice shakes despite my best intentions. Even though my feelings toward X-13 are complicated, I'm not sure I like the idea of him haunting my dreams for the rest of my life.

Dr. Wright shakes her head. "The effect has always faded

with time and distance."

I take a deep breath and nod. "So what does it mean?" I ask. When Wright looks to Director Ramsey for an answer, my anxiety cranks back up to eleven again. "Is he actually there? In my dreams? Can he— it—"

"It can't hurt you, if that's what you're worried about," Dr. Wright says. "There is no evidence that it can affect you physically. But there does appear to be some sort of…mental connection, or bridge, that allows it to visit your dreams."

"So it can see me and hear me in them?" I ask, wanting to be sure. They're being frustratingly vague, and this is more important to me than I can admit. "Will it remember the things that I dream?"

"Yes," Director Ramsey answers, and the way he looks at me brings up memories of old, bitter teachers who never liked me. "It will remember the things you reveal, the things you dream. Your fears and your secrets. It will use them against you if it can."

I clasp my hands in my lap and try to control my expression as my body goes hot with shame, then cold with fear. If it's secrets the Nightmare is hungry for, I've *created* one by giving in to my nighttime fantasies. Not to start with the moral implications of me consorting with a lab subject. I never would've done what I did if I had the faintest inkling it was *real*. It makes me frustrated all over again that Wright and the others waited until now to tell me.

Then again, I guess they couldn't have imagined that I'd decide to get down and dirty with a living nightmare. They've probably never encountered my particular brand of Fucked Up before.

I clear my throat and try to change the subject. "So how

would you like me to proceed, given this new information?"

"We're not making any changes to your instructions for the moment," Ramsey says. "Continue as usual until you hear otherwise from us."

I nod while thinking there is no chance in hell that's happening.

* * *

I leave the room alone to head back to my lab for the remainder of the workday, eager to get some privacy so I can have a meltdown in peace. But I soon hear the click of heels following me. I glance over my shoulder at Dr. Wright and slow down so she can catch up. Her expression is mild and her steps unhurried, as if she doesn't care whether she walks at my side. But once she's there, she looks sideways at me, gives me a small smile, and says. "You're doing well."

The praise is almost more shocking than the information I learned in that room. I blink at her dumbly. She continues, "Director Ramsey would never admit as such, of course, but he's pleased with how you're performing. We all are."

"How is that? I've just been following instructions."

"So you have," she says. "And that in itself is remarkable. Everyone else in your position has resigned within a couple weeks, complaining of recurring nightmares, sleep loss, and pervasive anxiety."

I frown. Though my first couple of dreams about the Nightmare were unsettling, since then I wouldn't describe them as particularly frightening. And I have been sleep deprived, but not any more anxious than normal. "Is it strange to admit I'm not scared of the subject?" I ask, lowering my voice and glancing around. Even though I doubt she could guess the full truth of how I've felt toward the Nightmare, it feels like a strange thing to say. Like something is wrong with me, some key component missing. *Crazy*, whispers a voice in the back of my mind that sounds uncomfortably like Ethan. "It feels like…like it's not really *trying* to scare me either. I don't know how to explain it."

Dr. Wright gives me a long, searching look. Again, I have the uncomfortable feeling that she knows more than she lets on. But it must be my self-consciousness. How could she possibly know? "Well, whatever you're doing, it's working," she says. "Keep it up. And my advice? Keep the details to yourself. Director Ramsey is impressed by your 'fortitude.'" She says the word like she knows it's not true. "Especially because of your…*feminine proclivities*." She rolls her eyes, and I bite back a grin at the open contempt. "That can only work in your favor."

I nod slowly, understanding what she's telling me and grateful for the advice. She didn't have to do this. And I feel like I understand her better now. Maybe she only seems cold because she has to, in this line of work. I can't imagine what kind of bullshit she has to put up with working for a man like Ramsey only for him to start favoring Ethan over her, even though she's undoubtedly been working here much longer. And during that conversation, I didn't get the impression she had told Ramsey or anyone else about my visit to her house and that embarrassing chat we had, which I'm grateful for. "I appreciate it, Dr. Wright."

She gives me another thin sliver of a smile. "Calliope is fine."

I smile back. "All right. Thanks, Calliope."

She continues on down the hallway with a swish of her skirt and the click of heels, leaving me feeling surprisingly comforted. At least I know I'm not entirely alone in this place.

Chapter Seventeen

That sort-of tribunal was so stressful that the rest of the day is a blur. My lunch gets pushed later, so I eat alone in an empty break room, taking mechanical bites of my sandwich. Still, even as I run through my instructions for the day and do my damnedest not to make eye contact with the Nightmare, I can't fight the nagging feeling that I'm forgetting something.

While I'm lying in bed on my phone that night, it finally occurs to me. If the dreams have been real this whole time… then the Nightmare *has* communicated with me. It's spoken to me. Demonstrated intelligence and sentience. We've had whole conversations. And much more than conversations.

Which means that Dr. Wright was fucking *lying* when she insisted the Nightmare wasn't an intelligent being.

I let my phone drop to the bed and glare at the ceiling. All of the warm things I felt toward her after that meeting bleed away. The Nightmare *is* more intelligent than they originally let on. He has thoughts and feelings and a soul. No matter what else they say about him, or what he's done, that much is true.

And I've been ignoring him in real life while fucking him in my dreams. Using him like a *thing*.

I press my palms over my eyes, letting out a slow breath.

I feel stupid. So goddamn stupid. But after that humiliating experience with Dr. Wright, and the panel with the director and Ethan, I know better than to rush to confront anyone. Especially since revealing too much about my dreams with the Nightmare could lead to some…very uncomfortable conversations. My palms are sweating just thinking about it.

If I'm going to do this, I need to do this right. And that means, first, that I have to confront everything I've done wrong.

* * *

When I open my eyes again that night, in the dream version of my bedroom, I sit up slowly and clutch the sheets to my chest. Now that I know this is real, I wore a set of real pajamas to bed instead of my usual scanty clothing, but I still feel vulnerable.

Now that I'm properly paying attention, I'm not sure how I didn't notice that my dreams have been different, more real, ever since the Nightmare entered them. Not only do I always dream of my own bedroom, but it's far too accurate. In dreams, there are always little differences that make the environment strange, or break reality.

But here, everything is just like it is in real life.

Except for the Nightmare standing in one corner, watching me with those dark eyes. I slowly turn to look at him.

I can *feel* too much for this to be a normal dream too. Like the slide of my silken sheets in my fingers, the thump of my heartbeat in my chest. The flare of hot shame as I think about what I did in that last dream before Dr. Wright and the others told me the truth.

"I didn't know this was real," I whisper. "I'm sorry."

The Nightmare's head tilts, though the rest of him doesn't move, and his expression is unchanging. "For what?"

"What I did wasn't right."

"Why?" he asks. "You still believe I am less intelligent than you?" He grins, like the thought is funny to him. One clawed hand lifts and slowly moves through familiar motions: the sign language for my name.

I shake my head without having to think about it. It doesn't matter how much I've questioned myself or been lied to. If this plane of existence is real, then I have no doubt that the Nightmare is an intelligent being like I thought all along. More than just thoughts, he has feelings. Wants. But that only makes the reality of the situation more horrific.

"You're a prisoner," I say.

"Not here," he says. "Here, I choose to visit you."

My heart skips a beat. I want to ask more, ask *why*, but I can't let myself get distracted. "I heard you visit everyone who works with you in the lab."

He inclines his head. "True." His lips curl upward, a hint of sharp teeth showing through. "But those visits were very different from the ones I have had with you."

I flush, remembering the feeling of his huge hands cradling me, his teeth pricking my skin, and a whole medley of other sensations that I really shouldn't be thinking about right now. I swallow hard. "You only gave them nightmares." He did for me, too, but only at first.

"None of them fought back as you did," he says, clearly thinking back to the same encounters. "It made me respect you. And then…" His eyes rove over me in a way that makes heat curl in my lower belly. "You woke things in me that I have not felt for a very long time."

As his voice drops to a low, rough growl, I have to fight off the urge to relive that last, pleasurable visit. I can't. I press my thighs together as if I can contain my desire there. "It's not right for things to be like that between us," I insist. "Your physical body is still imprisoned. And I have power over you. It's fucked up."

"You are not the one who has me trapped," he says. His face shifts, and a moment later I find myself staring into the cold, lined features of Director Ramsey. I shudder, and he shifts back to normal.

"But you're still trapped," I argue. "It's still not right—"

His eyes flash. Darkness writhes around him, tendrils stretching his form into something far larger and less humanoid. A mass of writhing darkness overtaking the room. "No. It is not," he says, voice dark and echoing. But a moment later, he calms, and his body slowly shrinks back to his humanoid form. "But it is not your fault either. And here..." I blink, and suddenly, he's looming over the bed, looking down at me, stretching to seven feet tall again. "Here I have the power."

Even when he's showing off like this, I don't feel an urge to cower. Instead, I scowl up at him.

"You said it was my dream," I say.

He grins. "I lied. Sorry, little dreamer."

All the more reason that I should fear him. He's called the Nightmare for a reason. He's killed people. Driven others to nervous breakdowns. And yet...he has never harmed me. Even at the beginning, he only tried to frighten me, and that didn't last long. "So you're trying to say...we're even?" I ask, gnawing my lip as I consider the prospect. I can't deny that he has a point. There's still a power imbalance of sorts between us, but it's a twisted one, not as clear-cut as a captor and prisoner, experimenter and experiment.

"I am saying…" He leans over, and one claw delicately tucks a strand of hair behind my ear. I stare up at him, eyes wide, unable to look away. "There is a connection between us. Something I have not felt with another human."

His huge, clawed hand hovers near my face, and I slowly lean over to press my cheek against his palm. I feel so cradled, so safe, despite the deadly tips of each claw. Maybe I'm a fool, but I can't help it. I trust him. I feel safe when I'm here. "I feel something too," I murmur, breathing in that delicious scent of smoke and pepper. "My mind says I shouldn't. But…that doesn't stop me from feeling the way I do."

"You humans rely too much on logic," the Nightmare says. One hand still on my face, he grabs my waist with the other and pulls me toward him with effortless strength to set me on his lap. I lean against him, sighing at the sensation of being enfolded within his velvety darkness.

"You should instead trust your instincts," he says. "Those are what truly keep you alive." His hand shifts to the back of my head, and I bury my face against his chest, breathing deep. He smells like smoke and spice, like wood and wild. I did not know anything could smell so distinct in a dream—but then again, this is no ordinary dream, as I should've realized from the very start.

"My instincts…" I murmur against him.

"What do they tell you?"

I consider the question. Try to push aside my logic, if only for a moment. How do I feel with him? Safe. Cared for. I feel…a yearning. A connection, new and fragile but already more intense than any I've felt with any of my exes. But *that* feels dangerous, at odds with the sense of physical safety. My body is safe with the Nightmare, but my heart is not. I've worked so hard to protect that part of myself since Ethan hurt me, but I let down my walls with the Nightmare because I didn't think any of this was real at first.

I sigh, shutting my eyes and shaking my head. Indecision plagues me once again. "I think my instincts are as confused as the rest of me."

"No." I'm surprised by his curtness. Even more surprised when, a moment later, he abruptly shoves me back onto the bed and pins my wrists above my head, his snarling teeth just inches from my face. I let out a little cry of surprise, but I don't try to struggle. When my breath hitches, it's not with fear. After a moment, he pulls back and looks down at me with amusement.

"You see?" he asks. "Your body knows the truth. Your brain is what is making this complicated."

I squirm, then, frustrated. Of course, it doesn't get me anywhere. "Things aren't so simple," I argue.

"And why not?" He leans down, face pressing against the side of my neck.

I tense at the feeling of warm breath against my skin, my body aching with want despite my head's disagreement. "Because… It…" It's hard to think. I let out a small whimper as the sharp points of his teeth tease the skin of my neck—not in pain, but desire. The point of contact sends a wave of pleasure all the way through my body, intensifying into a throbbing at my core.

"Tell me, Mara," he whispers, long tongue flicking against

the sensitive skin behind my ear. "Am I the helpless one here?"

I swallow hard, squirming in his grip. "No," I whisper.

"No," he agrees in a pleased murmur. "Here, you are mine."

"I—" I start to protest, and he bites my neck, drawing a cry of shock out of me. It hurts, but the spark of pain soon turns into a confusing wave of pleasure as his tongue smooths over the place his teeth marked. "I— I—"

"Say it," he purrs, teeth scraping over the already-raw skin again.

My back arches, a low keening escaping my mouth. "I'm yours."

"Good girl." He pulls back enough that I can see his face and he can see mine, doubtlessly flushed, as my chest heaves for air and my wrists strain uselessly against his grip. "Now tell me what you want."

"I…" I shut my eyes, but at his growl of disapproval, I open them again and look up at him. His own eyes are intense, burning as they lock onto mine. "I want…"

"Louder," he says, squeezing my wrists so hard, it's almost painful.

"I want everything," I gasp out. "Anything. All you can give me." It's incoherent, babbling, but it's true no matter how humiliating it is to admit. I want him to taste me and bite me and hurt me. I want him to fuck me so hard, I can barely walk in the morning. I want to give myself entirely to him. "I want *you*," I say, unsure how to put all of that into words without sounding desperate.

His lips slowly curl into a sharp-edged smile. "Then you shall have me," he says.

But instead of pinning me down and fucking me hard, the way I want, he grips me by the wrists and dangles me above the bed. I gasp and squirm. Holy God, he is *strong*. It hurts a little, being held like this. But much more than that, it turns me on. He watches me, gauging my reaction before he begins to undress me.

It's maddeningly slow. One piece of clothing at a time. He tugs down my long pajama pants and tosses them aside. My shirt comes off next; he maneuvers my body expertly while I remain limp and let him do as he pleases. He leaves me like that for a moment, eyes roving over my breasts and the smooth expanse of my stomach before a shadowy tendril reaches for my panties. It forms a tentacle-like shape and rubs over the already-damp fabric, providing tantalizing friction over my clit, until I let out a helpless little moan. Only then does he pull the panties down and toss them aside, leaving me fully naked and helpless in front of him.

I flush despite myself. He's fucked me before, but it was different then. I didn't know it was real. Now I feel more exposed, more self-conscious. I press my thighs together, averting my gaze from his intense stare. But a moment later, two shadowy tentacles wrap around my thighs and force them apart hard enough that I gasp. Another grabs me by the chin and forces my face back up toward him.

"You are beautiful," he says.

I want to turn away, but instead I hold his gaze. Something bold and hungry sparks in my chest. I already showed him the desires I've always been ashamed of…and he was eager to fulfill them. I swallow hard. "Then maybe you should do something more than stare at me," I challenge in a whisper.

He chuckles. While the shadows hold me in place, he moves forward until he's kneeling on the bed in front of my dangling form.

"I will not be rushed," he murmurs. He presses his shadowy lips to my ankle, my calf, my thigh, slow and unhurried. I try to squirm, but the tentacles only tighten their grip, spreading my thighs obscenely wide. When he smiles up at me from between my legs, I am laid bare—trembling and glistening with need.

"Please," I whimper, and his grin grows.

"Please what, Mara?"

Fucker. I bite my lip, warring with my self-consciousness, and then finally whisper, "Please…eat me."

His smile turns hungry. He presses another kiss to my inner thigh, agonizingly close to where I ache with desire, and then that deliciously long tongue snakes out of his mouth and slides against my skin. I groan, chest heaving, as he teases at one thigh, and then the other. Each time inching a little bit higher, but never reaching where I need him.

"Please," I beg again, writhing as much as his grip on me allows. "God, please—" I cut off with a gasp of pleasure as his warm tongue finally slides against me. He hums in pleasure, and I feel it vibrate in my core. He licks me slowly, from ass to clit, and then his tongue flicks against that sensitive bud and I whimper again.

"You taste so good," he murmurs, his hot breath ghosting against my sensitive skin.

"Then don't *stop*," I gasp, too turned on to worry about how needy I sound.

He huffs a laugh and resumes, his tongue lapping at me in long, smooth motions, teasing me until I am dripping wet and painfully sensitive. I whimper and beg and twist in the grip of the shadows still holding me helpless in the air. And finally, just when the teasing has become painful, he devotes his full attention to my clit, tongue swirling with slowly increasing pressure, exhaling a moan against me as though this is as pleasurable for him as it is for me. That liquid heat inside of me boils over and I come hard against his mouth, whimpering with pleasure, grinding against his tongue to wring out every last drop of satisfaction. He doesn't pull back until I stop shaking, and then looks up at me and licks his sharp teeth.

Just as the ripples of my orgasm fade, he presses his mouth to me again and his tongue dips inside of me. I gasp at the new sensation, back arching as his long, serpentine tongue slides in, and in, and in, stuffing me almost as full as his cock can. I am still achingly sensitive after my first orgasm, but now that pleasure cranks back up to eleven, almost overwhelmingly good.

"Oh fuck," I breathe. His tongue twists, striking that sweet spot, and I let out an incoherent cry of pleasure. He strokes me again and again, until it is riding on the edge of being too intense. I come again, so hard that my vision goes dark around the edges, writhing and shuddering in his grip. He doesn't stop until I go limp, chest heaving as I pant. He pulls back, his tongue slowly receding back into his mouth, and presses a wet kiss to the inside of my thigh.

His shadowy tendrils lower me to the bed, where I lay boneless and hollowed out with pleasure. My Nightmare curls himself around me like a warm blanket, claws stroking delicately through my hair, and holds me until the morning light leaks through the window.

I blink and wake up alone in my bed, but his warmth lingers on my skin.

Chapter Eighteen

During the next couple of weeks, I fall into a routine. During the day, I attend work like normal, running through my instructions with as much unbiased precision as I can muster. I try to embrace the monotony of work and not think about my dreams. But one way or another, the Nightmare seems to always occupy my thoughts. The only exception is my lunch break every day, where Belle has started to join me and Ezra. His good humor slowly draws her out of her shell, and the three of us strike up an easy friendship.

And at night, in my dreams, I am visited by the same monster I'm studying during the day. Sometimes he talks to me in my bedroom. Other nights, he chases me down the hallways in a playful callback to our first terrifying encounter. Either way, we usually end up tangled together, breathless and sweaty, while he coaxes pleasure out of my body in ways I didn't know possible. Teeth and claws and tongue and tentacles, and a cock that always fills me perfectly. Every morning I wake sweaty and sated and alone.

I know this situation is fucked up. Maybe I should be frightened when his huge, clawed hands pin me to the wall, or his sharp teeth prick my exposed throat. But I'm not.

Especially since he's giving me the best orgasms of my life.

The only part I regret is that he is still trapped in his cell. The Nightmare doesn't complain about it, and seems content by the freedom offered by our nighttime escapades, but my consternation only grows as I spend more time with him. I don't care what the director or Dr. Wright say, the Nightmare is no mindless monster or vicious beast. He is a conscious being who does not deserve to be caged and experimented on. More than that, he is caring and compassionate and intelligent. I *feel* it whenever I'm with him.

"I wish there was a way for me to prove that you're not just some *thing*," I murmur as we lie tangled together one night, my body pleasantly wrapped up by his tendrils of shadows.

"It does not matter to me," he says, nuzzling against the side of my neck. "They will never see me as anything but a monster."

"That's just because they're not looking hard enough," I grumble.

He pauses and sighs. "I must admit, I have given them little reason to see me for who I am. I have been…angry, in the past. I have made mistakes."

The sorrow in his voice gives me pause and makes me remember those photographs Dr. Wright showed me when I first brought up the issue of the Nightmare's sentience. I've tried to forget those horrible sights as I've grown closer to the Nightmare, but now a flicker of doubt wriggles its way into my heart. I turn onto my side so I can look at him face-to-face.

"They showed me some things," I say, studying his expression. "Bodies. They said…said you killed people."

Part of me hopes he will deny it. Even if it's a lie, perhaps I could bring myself to believe it. But the Nightmare only nods, regret flickering behind his eyes. "As I said," he whispers. "I was angry. And past experimenters were not as kind as you are." His eyebrows draw together. "I attempted to escape. I was willing to do anything." He looks away, shame evident in his shadowy features. "I hurt people. Killed them. Some of them had not harmed me; they were only in my way. I did not care."

I draw in a shaky breath. It's hard to hear…but I can't entirely blame him. If I were trapped in a cell unfairly for decades, poked and prodded and tortured, unable to even communicate properly with the people keeping me there, wouldn't I be desperate to escape? Willing to do horrible things for freedom?

I gently turn his face toward me.

"That still doesn't make you a monster," I murmur. "There are plenty of people who have done things just as bad, with far less excuses." I press my forehead to his. "It doesn't mean you deserve what's being done to you."

"Maybe," he says like he doesn't really believe it. Before I can argue, he continues, "But I have given up on the idea of escape." He reaches with a shadowy hand and cups the back of my head. His palm is large enough to cradle my entire skull. "Especially now that I have my nights with you. This is enough. More than enough."

The way he's holding me rekindles the heat in my lower body. Goddamn, I'm not sure I'll ever have enough of him, but I force myself to focus on the conversation at hand because it's important. "But it's not fair," I say. "If you were free now, you wouldn't hurt anyone, would you?"

"No," he says. "I never did before I was trapped against my will. It is not in my nature. My kind—we do thrive on fear, on nightmares, but not real pain. Not death. There is nothing to gain from it." He's never spoken about his kind before, and it makes me so curious to know more, but I hold my tongue because it's clear he has more to say. His expression is thoughtful, like he's really considering my question. "And I understand humans now. I know that many are kind. I have no desire to hurt them." He tilts his head, considering. "I mean, unless perhaps you wanted me to. Or if someone were to hurt you." His expression darkens, and so does the room around us as his shadowy tendrils spread out over the bed. His body grows, claws sharpening and teeth lengthening as he snarls. "Then I would rip their head off of their body and—"

"Okay, okay, enough!" I nudge him playfully, and in an instant, he snaps back into his normal humanoid form. "Definitely don't say that if the director or someone asks you," I say. Though, honestly, it makes me feel pleased to hear. Some dark part of me is thrilled by the idea of having someone who will do anything to protect me. *My own personal monster*, I think fondly, even though I know he's much more than that. "I think the people who work at the Facility should know what they're doing. They should understand more about you. I think… I mean, if I explain it properly, they'd have to let you go, right? Or at least give you more freedom, more rights. They wouldn't keep you locked up there if they knew what you were really like. They couldn't."

Even as I say it, *wanting* it to be true, cold doubt worms into my head. I'd be stupid to believe that people like Ethan or Dr. Ramsey would do the right thing. Maybe they *do* know. But…it can't be true of everyone who works there, and it certainly can't be true of the whole outside world. If they won't do the right thing on principle, I'll have to find a way to make them.

The Nightmare lets out a doubtful grumble, but I ignore it and push on. "And I think I can gather the evidence. What do you say?"

He is silent for several long seconds, and I wonder if he's going to refuse, if he's too jaded to feel the same spark of hope that I feel. But then, finally, he dips his chin in a nod. "If that is what you want," he says.

He doesn't sound confident. But that's fine, all the more reason for me to prove him wrong. I can't wait for the day I get to open his cell and meet him in the real world. But for now, I grin and playfully pin him down on the bed as I shift to straddle him.

"Good monster," I tease, leaning down to kiss him. "Now… do that thing with the tentacles again." I grin wickedly. "Please."

* * *

This time, I'm going to do this right. I'm not going to leave any room for doubt. And dealing with people like Dr. Wright and Director Ramsey means gathering too much evidence for them to hand-wave away. Especially since I think they know, or at least suspect, the truth. It must be inconvenient, finding out that the monster you've been keeping captive for decades is actually a thinking, feeling, living being…but I'm not going to let them pretend they don't realize exactly what they're doing. If they're confronted with cold, hard facts showing that the Nightmare is conscious and reasonable, they'll have no choice but to listen to me, and to do something about this fucked-up situation.

Unfortunately, the rules of the building make it very hard for me to gather the evidence I need. I'm not authorized to take photos, or videos, or notes beyond the ones I turn in at the end of every day. And if I leave my notes overnight, I'm afraid that they'll find them too early and try to stop me. They could simply bury the truth, fire me, and I'll be left with nothing. I have no illusions about the type of people I'm dealing with here; this place has been shady from the start, everyone has lied to me, and I'm kicking myself for being complacent for so long. I will no longer be an accessory to their cruelty.

So if making things right requires a little bit of rule breaking, then so be it. It's a risk I'm willing to take. A risk I *have* to take, for the sake of freeing the Nightmare from his captivity.

The next time a weekend rolls around, I initiate my plan. First, I tell my parents that I'm going on a daytrip to visit an old high school friend in the nearby town of Yuma. I borrow my mom's car and "forget" my phone at home in case the Facility is tracking it. I don't even bring my vape, to be extra *extra* safe. Then I drive to an entirely different town and ditch the car to catch a taxi paid in cash. Maybe I'm being paranoid, but I don't know how far the Facility's reach extends, or how far they're willing to go to protect their secrets. I can't take any chances.

Next, I buy a burner phone—also with cash—and connect it to a secure Cloud on a local library's computer. And, since I don't want to access these files at all while I'm at home, I type up some preliminary notes in the Cloud while I'm there. I write out everything I know about the Nightmare's history, his behavior during my time at the Facility, and his appearances in my dreams. I lay it all bare, including our intimacy—without the dirty details, of course.

Nobody needs to know about my proclivity for tentacles or the things that long tongue can do.

When I read them over, the notes sound a little like the

ravings of a lunatic. A desperate girl in love with a monster. I think again of all those times Ethan called me *crazy*, *obsessive*, and bite the inside of my cheek, hating that a wave of doubt rushes over me. Is that what I'm doing right now? Going off the deep end?

But no. *No.* I *know* I'm right, and I'm not going to let anyone convince me otherwise. The Nightmare is counting on me, and I will not let him down. My words won't be enough, but my evidence will prove everything.

Thus the need for the phone. Now, I have a cell with no trail and a way to upload the evidence. The next step is to figure out a way to sneak it into the Facility.

I already feel like a criminal, and perhaps a completely insane person, doing all of this. But I reassure myself that it's all for a good cause. The Nightmare does not deserve to be trapped in that tiny, bare cell and experimented on. I will do whatever it takes to free him, even if it means burning my life to the ground.

After some fervent internet research—again on a public library computer—I head to work on Monday with a plan.

Step one: hide the phone in a potted plant just outside the entrance to the facility.

Step two: leave my normal phone with the guard, along with the jewelry I wore today just for this occasion.

"I'm going out right after work today," I explain when the guard squints at the over-the-top, shiny metal earrings. He grunts and waves me through.

Then I go through the metal detectors and work the rest of the day as normal, even though every time I think about what I'm about to do, it feels like my heart is trying to fight its way out of my chest.

At the end of the day, it's time for step three. I gather my phone and other belongings, put my jewelry back on, walk out of the building, and collect my burner phone while the guard is distracted. I hesitate a moment and then rush back into the building. Time for step four, when things get dangerous.

"Um, I'm so sorry," I say, flashing my brightest, most charming smile at the sour-faced guard. "I actually really have to go to the bathroom. Do you mind if I run back through just for a second?"

The man doesn't look happy about it, but after a moment he grumbles, "Yeah, just hand over the phone."

"Thanks so much," I say, dropping my regular cell phone into his hand without hesitation and rushing through the metal detectors. They send off their beeping alarms, but I whirl, give an apologetic smile, and point at my jewelry. There's a heart-stopping moment as the man squints at me. Then he waves a dismissive hand and barks, "Hurry up."

I sprint to the bathroom, heart pounding. Last step: I hide the cell phone in a plastic bag in the top compartment of a toilet and then head back out. The metal detectors go off again, *only* for my earrings this time. I collect my phone and suppress my triumphant grin until I turn my back on the building. The burner phone is officially inside the Facility.

* * *

The next morning, when I head into work, the phone is waiting for me in the bathroom. As I slip it into my pocket and head into the observation lab, I feel both absurdly proud of my criminal masterminding and also scared witless. I have no delusions about how much trouble I could get into for pulling this stunt. I'd *definitely* be fired, and probably face legal consequences.

But as I sit in my observation chair, open the viewing panel, and look in at the Nightmare sitting on the edge of his bed and waiting for me in his human form, I know I've made the right decision. I need to help him; I am the only one who can.

I have to be very careful about this part too. I need compelling, solid evidence to prove that the Nightmare is sentient. Photos, notes, and videos. Not only do I need data that will convince Director Ramsey and other higher-ups in the facility, but I need proof that will also hold up in the court of public opinion if they give me no choice but to release it to the world. It can't look like it was photoshopped or anything like that.

I also can't deviate too far from my usual work routine. I still need to make it through my daily to-do list to avoid arousing suspicion, and they've been increasing my workload, so it's not so easy. Plus, there's the camera in the back of the room.

Luckily, the Nightmare and I have every night to scheme together, planning for how to pull this off quickly and efficiently. We've plotted it all, and he's been practicing his sign language. We are able to work together like a well-oiled machine. He gives me performative reactions to the usual stimuli, rushing through the daily work. As soon as I bring down the privacy screen, he knows it's time for us to collect some evidence. I keep my back angled to the camera and the phone hidden in front of me, and snap some photos and videos of him in various forms, with focus on his humanoid one. I know that will be the most compelling for people, just like it was for me.

Then—keeping my phone tucked discreetly into a sleeve—I

record some conversations. I speak aloud and then translate his sign language. This part was not planned out because I didn't want any chance of it coming off scripted.

"Hello, Mr. Nightmare," I say. He smiles like I thought he would. I can practically hear the dark chuckle that features so often in my dreams.

Hello, Mara, he signs back at me while I translate aloud.

"Today, I'd like to record some basic proof of your logical capabilities," I say.

Yes, ma'am.

For the first day, I keep things simple. I have him count to thirty and then back. I have him perform some basic math and spelling. Of course, he has to add his own bit of dramatic flair, sometimes writing out the answers in tendrils of shadows, often rolling his eyes in exasperation when I ask him something he deems too simple.

It's good. It's gold. I don't know how anyone could watch this and not believe that he's as capable of thought and feeling as they are. But I know it's not enough. Still, not wanting to get too greedy and attract attention, I call it a day and head home feeling satisfied.

* * *

The next day, I go through the motions again, and then decide to dig a little deeper. Nobody has confronted me for unusual activity yet, so I assume I'm getting away with it so far.

"You told me once that you have many names," I say, propping my chin up with one hand and holding the phone with the other. The Nightmare sits on the other side of the glass in his own chair made of shadow, imitating my posture. "But you wouldn't tell me what they are. Will you tell me now?"

He blinks. He clearly wasn't expecting this question, but after a moment he nods. *Some have called me Epiales*, he says, carefully spelling out the name. *Others, Somnus.*

"Somnus," I repeat in a whisper. "I like that one. Could I call you that from now on?"

He nods. Then his gaze goes a little distant, and I'm dying to ask for more details about what he's remembering, but he surprises me by saying, *I have also been called Mara, in fact.*

"What?" Now I'm the one who's surprised. I almost forget to translate, and then hurriedly do so in order to continue with the conversation. "Really?"

Yes. In Old Norse. It was a word for a creature that brought nightmares.

"Ah. Like an old-school sleep paralysis demon," I say, remembering the research I did in our early days together. It feels very far away now.

"Is that what you are, then? Are you a demon?" I ask it playfully, but my stomach gives a nervous little twist as I realize I'm not sure how he'll respond.

But he shakes his head vehemently. *Not demon.*

"But you do bring nightmares. Why?"

He pauses, looking thoughtful. *I do not know*, he says, and then frowns, frustrated, clearly trying to think of a way to communicate what he wants to say.

"It is in my…heart?" I translate, tilting my head. "Are you saying…it is just your nature?"

He nods, relief clear in his features.

"I understand," I say. "Some would call what you do malicious." Again I sense that I'm treading on dangerous ground, but I need to do this. I'm trying to prove not only that the Nightmare is conscious and intelligent, but that he is not a threat or a monster that people should be afraid of. It's true that he has sins to atone for, but that doesn't mean he deserves to be locked up in a windowless room and experimented on for the rest of his life. I'm not sure if he can ever be integrated fully into human society, but I'm certain he deserves better than he gets in this place. And as he told me, he never harmed anyone until he was forced into captivity here. "Do you hate humans?"

No! He signs vehemently and frowns at me. *Nightmares are part of life. Necessary.* His shoulders lift in a silent sigh, and he struggles again to express what he wants to say through his limited sign language.

"Fear is human," I mutter, and then, "*To* fear is *to be* human, is that what you want to say?" He nods. "I think you're right. And nightmares don't really hurt us. A common theory is that they even help prepare us for the real dangers of the physical world."

He nods, then flashes me a sudden, wicked grin that gets my heart pounding. *Some people enjoy fear.*

"So does that mean you can bring good dreams too?" I ask, trying to keep us on task.

For you? Yes. Very good dreams.

Face heating up, I shut off the video.

After all, the quicker I get back home, the quicker I can fall asleep and show him exactly how I feel about *that*.

* * *

Even though work is exciting enough to garner all of my attention, my weekends are starkly empty, aside from occasional visits to Cup o' Happy in the morning. My parents notice how often I hole up in my room at home, just passing the time with TV shows and social media until I'm ready to sleep. I can tell that they're concerned. I promise them I'm making friends at work, but as another Saturday rolls around, I find myself at a loss again.

I know they're right. I can't spend my whole life alternating between work and dreams, even though I want to. Sometimes it feels like real life pales in comparison to my time with the Nightmare. *Somnus*, as I've taken to calling him in our more intimate moments. But that's no way to live.

I need to do *something* tonight, if only to reassure my parents I'm not sinking into the deep, dark abyss of depression. But I'm not too keen on trying my hand at the Dustpan again, especially if it means running into Ethan. I could video chat with Amy and my other college buddies, but given the distance, our friendship has been reduced to mostly emojis on social media. Now that I'm considering staying in Ash Valley for a while, I need to build a life *here*. So, on a whim, I shoot a text over to Belle and Ezra, inviting them out for a casual dinner.

A couple hours later, I'm seated in a plasticky red corner booth at a local diner with them. I'm weirdly nervous and changed my outfit three times. We hang out for an hour every workday at lunch, but this is my first time meeting them outside of the Facility, other than that one unfortunate bar night with Belle.

Even dressed casually, with Belle in a cute floral minidress and Ezra in an anime tee and skinny jeans, they still stand out in the small-town vibes of this place. They both seem relieved when I join them in the booth.

"I drive by this place every day but I've never been inside," Ezra says, perusing the laminated and slightly sticky menu with an enthusiasm the place does not deserve.

"Really?" I raise a brow. "I'm surprised. It's the okay-est restaurant in town."

"We're not really encouraged to mingle with the locals," he says, shrugging. "I mean, not that I particularly care about that sort of thing, but it was suggested that they might not be, ah, too friendly toward out-of-towners?"

"Mm. I guess we don't get too many new faces around here." I wish I could argue that Ash Valley is a welcoming place, but I'm not so sure it's the truth. Even now, I notice eyes lingering on Ezra and Belle. The latter especially seems hyperaware of it, nervously twirling a strand of hair around one finger and barely speaking a word since she's arrived. "Especially because most of them work at the Facility, and people are a bit…superstitious about it."

Both of them nod their understanding. Belle in a nervous sort of way, Ezra more of an *eh, what can you do?*

Truthfully, knowing what I do about the Facility, I can't blame the locals for their trepidation. The place is even weirder than most of them likely suspect. If they knew about the monsters housed on the outskirts of their town… I suppress a little shudder at the thought. Ash Valley isn't an *entirely* backwards place, but I can't say with complete confidence that they wouldn't be willing to pick up some pitchforks and run the director and his ilk out of town, either. Nor that I could blame them for it.

"But you're here with me, a born-and-bred Ash Valleyan," I say encouragingly, meeting Belle's eyes and offering a smile.

"And, who knows, with me and Ethan working there, maybe we'll finally start to build some bridges between the Facility and the local populace. Dr. Wright told me that was one of her goals."

Belle seems heartened by that. Still, when the waitress comes by to take our orders—waffles for me, a veggie burger for Belle, and nearly bloody steak for Ezra, along with a margarita for each of us—it's impossible to ignore that the employee only speaks directly to me throughout the interaction, even with Ezra being teeth-achingly polite.

I sigh when she's gone, propping an elbow up on the table and resting my chin on my hand. "Oh, well. They'll thaw out eventually. They're not unfriendly, really, just a little skittish."

"Can't imagine the facility has the greatest track record of dealing with locals either," Ezra says. "Especially with folks like Dr. Wright and the director acting as the face of the place."

"God, can you imagine Dr. Wright eating at a place like this?" I ask, grinning at the image. Ezra lets out a hearty laugh, and Belle cracks a tiny smile.

The mood lightens from there, especially once the margaritas arrive. The glasses are almost the size of my head, and the bartender is known for a heavy pour. Belle is pink in the face after several sips.

"You have no idea how good it feels to hang out with people I haven't known since grade school," I say, heaving a sigh and taking another hearty swig of my drink. "That's my least favorite thing about this place. Everyone already knows who I am. It feels like I grew up so much when I got out of here, but now that I'm back, it'd be so easy to fall back into old habits."

"I get that," Ezra says. "Though this place is hard to navigate as an outsider too. Especially since the nature of our work is so…isolating."

I nod, sympathetic. It's hard, holding that kind of a secret inside of you. Even now, there are blank spots in the conversation that we have to talk circles around, none of us quite sure how much we're allowed to say about our work.

But after some time passes and our glasses empty, we slip into easy conversation. I learn that Belle is an aspiring marine biologist from Florida and that she was approached personally by Dr. Wright shortly after she graduated from college. Her thesis was on the possible existence of real mermaids, or a creature that inspired their folklore, which garnered Wright's attention. It makes me oh-so-curious about what kind of subject Belle is working with—*are* mermaids real, after all?—but I bite my tongue, since I know that's something she won't be able to answer.

Ezra, on the other hand, hails from the Bay Area and was a cognitive science major. Rather than his schooling gathering the attention of the Facility, he attributes their job offer to his side hustle: a popular podcast about ghosts and hauntings. He, too, was approached directly. I have the sense that he's caught glimpses of a wider range of the Facility's creatures than Belle or I have, and it takes all my willpower not to beg for hints about what he's seen there.

The whole thing makes me so curious about how they run things at the Facility. It seems that Dr. Wright and company track down well-educated folks with an interest in the paranormal or folklore and recruit them. It makes sense for their type of work; they need science backgrounds to study the natures of these creatures, but they also need open minds who are willing to expand their ideas of what reality entails.

It does make me wonder how deep the rabbit hole goes.

That facility is huge, and it's been around forever. Who knows what else they house there? Belle's background hints at the existence of something like mermaids, and the Nightmare is even stranger, so how much folklore could be real? Vampires, shapeshifters, werewolves, ghosts... God only knows what's real and what's not at this point.

Chapter Nineteen

When I walk into work the next day, I stop short as I see a familiar, unwelcome face waiting in the lobby. Director Ramsey looks as stern as he did during my uncomfortable interrogation a couple of weeks ago. I haven't seen him since then, so his presence now does not bode well. Am I in trouble? Did they discover my burner phone, or notice me using it on the security camera? I swallow hard and try to walk normally past him, but he looks up and catches my eye, and I lurch to a stop.

"Ms. Vance," he says, his serious tone sending a flare of panic through me. "I'm going to observe your work today."

"I… What? Observe? Today?" Oh God. I'm parroting him like an idiot. I snap my mouth shut before I can say anything stupid and bob my head up and down.

He follows me to room 13. I walk slowly, to stall and attempt to calm my racing heart before we're trapped in a room together. He can't have noticed what I'm doing, right? Surely, he would have called me out immediately or had security escort me right out. Have I been slacking on my day-to-day tasks? I don't think so. He said they were pleased with my work last time I saw him, didn't he? Well, he didn't, but Dr.

Wright did. Is he really going to sit and watch me all day while I run through boring instructions and take notes? It must be a waste of his time, observing the observers…

I try not to panic as I use my security card to open the room. I hold the door open for him and then stop awkwardly, realizing there's only one chair in here.

"Oh, um, do you…?" I look at him, unsure what I'm even trying to say.

He stands with his back to the wall and folds his arms over his chest. "I'm fine right here," he says.

I sit, feeling more awkward than ever. This is like having a teacher breathing down my neck while I was taking a test. I'm breaking into a cold sweat. God, why am I panicking? If he notices, he'll *know* I have something to be guilty about. At least he showed up before I retrieved the burner phone from the bathroom; there's no condemning evidence in the room with us. I just have to play it cool. It takes all of my effort to not let my eyes linger on Somnus through the observation panel, trying to silently warn him about what's happening.

Come on, brain, cut it out, I argue with myself as I pick up today's packet of instructions with trembling hands.

When I scan the first few items on the list, I relax. It doesn't look any different than my normal day-to-day instructions. Maybe this isn't the trap that it feels like, just a normal observation of my everyday work. It's possible that the director does this for every new hire at some point. It doesn't have to be a malicious visit, even though it still makes the hairs on the back of my neck rise to have him standing against the wall and watching me.

His eyes burn holes in the back of my head as I take a deep breath and start going through the daily tasks. I dutifully press buttons and record my notes on the Nightmare's responses while the director stares at me. My hands are shaky, and I'm slower than usual in my effort not to make any stupid mistakes, but otherwise, things seem to be going fine.

Somnus—the *Nightmare*, the subject, I remind myself, because it feels dangerous even to think his name here—performs his duty just like I am. His responses are boring, predictable, just like we've discussed while planning. I assume he must be puzzled why I'm not taking down the privacy screen and speaking to him like I normally do, but he goes along with me. Trusting me.

Just as I'm starting to relax, and think this day might not be so terrible after all, I reach the fifth item on my to-do list. *Record response to Sound 3.* For a moment, I'm not sure why that particular stimulus makes me hesitate.

Then it hits me. *Sound 3.* I remember that button. It was the one that drove me to my first attempt to communicate with the Nightmare, because I felt so goddamn guilty. I can still vividly recall the way he threw himself at the glass and writhed in pain, the way he had to pull himself together afterward. My stomach churns.

I swallow hard, folding my hands in my lap. My mind races to try to think of a way to decline this instruction without revealing far too much about myself and my relationship with Somnus.

"Respectfully, sir," I say, keeping my eyes trained on the form of the Nightmare instead of looking up at the director, "I already have detailed notes about the subject's adverse reaction to that particular stimulus."

Director Ramsey shifts his stance, spine stiffening. "I'm sure I don't need to lecture you about the necessity of repetition and proving replicability in scientific experiments."

I clench my hands, attempting to keep down my rising wave of anger. He knows exactly what he's doing. *Exactly* what he's asking of me. I'm sure of it. "Are there not notes on the same stimulus from my predecessors?" I ask, still trying to aim for politeness and logic. "I believe the subject's reaction to this sound to be extreme enough that it will taint any further tests, and surely there are better ways to spend this time—"

"Do not presume to tell me how to run my own facility," the director snaps, cutting me off. Any pretense of politeness is gone from his tone now; he's gone serious, icy, commanding. "I am not asking for your opinion on the matter, Ms. Vance. I am issuing a direct order, as your superior."

I picture the jaws of a bear trap snapping shut. I was right to be cautious after all—there is a reason for his visit, and I suspect this is it. He's testing me.

I take a deep breath and extend a shaking hand toward the button for Sound 3. I look at it instead of at Somnus. I know that he will understand when I explain it to him tonight. He would tell me that I should do what I must to maintain my job here, at least until I have the evidence I need to confront the director. Surely a few moments of agony is worse than us being forced apart, and the Nightmare being handed over to a new research assistant that will have no qualms about hurting him.

But...no matter what logic says, my hand stops short of the button. I can't bring myself to do it. I've already hurt Somnus before, when I didn't know any better, and the guilt still tears at me. I cannot do it again. I cannot knowingly hurt someone I care about.

My hand recoils from the button and returns to my lap. I

swallow and look up at the director. "No," I say. I don't plan to say it until it's out of my mouth. I don't care that I'm "just following orders," or that Somnus will understand. I'm not willing to hurt him, no matter what the consequences may be. "I won't."

Director Ramsey's brow furrows, his lips forming a firm line. I get the sense he's not used to hearing the word I just used. "You're refusing a direct order?" he asks, a challenge in his words.

I know where this is going. Still, I can't bring myself to budge. This is not a line I'm willing to cross. "Given that your order is immoral, yes, *sir*, I am."

His lips curl into a contemptuous shadow of a smirk. "Immoral," he repeats.

"Yes." My hands curl into fists in my lap. Even though I'm trying to keep my cool, I feel my anger starting to boil over. I hate that arrogant look on his face, the way he seems amused by my refusal, like this is some sort of game to him. "You're hurting him. You know you are. There's plenty of data on that test to prove it."

Just like that, the flicker of a horrible smile is gone. "*Him*? Are you referring to the subject? That thing within the cell?"

"Somnus is not a thing," I burst out before I can stop myself. There's a triumphant look in his eye that suggests I just gave him exactly what he was looking for, but still the words pour out of me. I've probably already lost my job, but if there's a chance I can make him understand, I have to take it. "He's not an animal either. He's smart, capable, and empathic. He is a being on the same level as you or me."

"Whatever romantic notions you've gotten into your head, I assure you, young lady, I know our subjects here far better than you do." The condescension in his voice makes my skin crawl.

My stomach sinks. Even though this is the first issue I've had here, I suspect I'm not a valuable enough employee to survive an incident like this. But I do have one trick up my sleeve still. And now, I have nothing left to lose. Before Ramsey can say a word, I lurch to my feet and glare up at him, fists clenched at my sides.

"Before you say more, I have something to show you," I say. "And trust me. You're going to want to see it." I take a deep breath, trying to steady myself. "Before the whole world does."

Chapter Twenty

I'm surprised that Director Ramsey agreed so readily to my demand. Either my threat worked, or he's eager to see the full hand I'm playing with. Or maybe he's looking for another chance to humiliate me. I'm standing back in what I think of as the Interrogation Room, where the director, Dr. Wright, and Ethan first told me that my dreams of Somnus are real.

But now I'm the one with secrets to reveal.

I keep telling myself that as I stand at the front of the room. Still, I can't shake the sense that I'm being interviewed, or interrogated, like the last time I was here. There's something vaguely humiliating about it, like I'm a child giving a presentation. But I force that feeling down and try to reassure myself. I *do* know what I'm doing. Perhaps I wasn't prepared for it to happen this way, but I have plenty of evidence on the burner phone I'm holding behind my back until we begin. Plus, I have the deep certainty that I am *right,* and nobody is going to take that from me this time. I just need to find the words to convince them.

Director Ramsey waits in his chair with his awful, condescending smirk. I hate looking at him, so I stare at the floor instead until Dr. Wright walks in the door.

"I hope you know what you're doing," she murmurs, brushing past me with barely a glance.

I clasp my shaky hands behind my back and take a deep breath. It doesn't matter if they already doubt me. I knew it would be an uphill battle, and I've worked hard to put together this evidence. I've made sure I have access to it on the Cloud too. So even if they don't believe me, it doesn't mean my fight is over.

Still, it'll be a whole lot easier for me if this works.

"When I first arrived at this facility," I begin once Dr. Wright takes her chair. My voice comes out steady; I may not have been fully prepared for this moment, but I do know what I want to say. What I *have* to say. "I was told that the subject I would be working with was no more intelligent than 'an average mammal.'" I pause, glancing between their faces, but their expressions betray nothing. "When I later raised concerns that perhaps this was not the case, I was given reassurances once again, and convinced that I was wrong." I meet Dr. Wright's eyes, and find a warning in them, but I'm long past heeding that. "After further work with X-13, the Nightmare, I have found thorough and compelling evidence that he is, in fact, much more than I was led to believe. He has shown a propensity for thought and emotion placing him on the same level of consciousness as any human being."

Director Ramsey sighs, and I falter, my next words dying on my tongue. He gives Dr. Wright an exasperated look, not even addressing me directly as he says, "Not another one of these. They *all* believe their monster is special. Didn't you deal with this?"

"Furthermore—" I butt in before she can answer, taking a

small step forward. I let my anger rise in my chest and bolster me. I will not be silenced or made small. I am *right*. "I have gathered evidence to prove my case."

Now I certainly have their attention. Dr. Wright's eyes widen while the director gives a confused frown.

"I assure you, we have gone over your extensive notes," Dr. Wright says. "There was nothing within that gave us reason to believe what you're saying is true." Again, her eyes flash in warning. A silent request not to do this.

Maybe I would have raised this with her privately if she hadn't already lied to me and made me feel like an idiot the first time I did it. No, I refuse to obey her now. I need to do this. I need to make myself impossible to ignore. So I look the director in the eyes instead of her, and continue.

"In addition to completing the tasks given to me, and conversing with the subject in my dreams, I have been conducting my own experiments. I have found that X-13 can communicate in the waking world as well."

"Impossible," the director says.

"I thought you might say as much." Now for the moment of truth. I'm sweating, anxious, but I don't let that stop me. I reach into my pocket and pull out the burner phone, and the room goes silent once more. "I have been collecting evidence. I have notes. Photos. Videos. Extensive recordings proving that what I am saying is true. He is clearly using sign language to communicate." I take a step forward with the phone in hand, and both Director Ramsey and Dr. Wright recoil as if I'm presenting them with a live snake. "If you'll allow me to show you—"

"That will not be necessary," the director says.

I open the phone anyway, pulling up a particular video file.

"Here, for example—"

On the phone, Somnus's clawed hand signs *Nightmares are part of life,* while I narrate aloud.

The director stands, marches around the table, and over to me. I shrink back but can't react fast enough as he grabs the burner phone from my hand and throws it to the tile. He stomps on it once, twice, a third time, grinding his heel into the shattered screen.

He's breathing hard when he's done, and I'm frozen in place. I can't believe he did that. I still have the cloud files, of course, but...the fact that he felt justified and safe in doing that doesn't bode well for any attempts to negotiate with him. I feel vaguely ill at the suddenness and ease of his anger. This man is volatile. Dangerous. I look pleadingly at Dr. Wright, still seated at the table, but the closes her eyes like she can't bear to look at me.

"Calliope," Director Ramsey says, his voice coming out strangely calm. She opens her eyes, head tilting slightly his way although she doesn't look directly at him. "There's no need to waste more of your time with this nonsense. Proceed with your duties. I will handle this..." His lip curls. "Nuisance."

This isn't good. But I know it would only make me look pathetic and weak if I ask Dr. Wright to stay. I try to beg her with my eyes—I *know* she knows I'm right—but she doesn't look at me. Her face is a cool mask as she nods at the director, stands, and heads for the exit. The room is silent except for the click of her heels. I force myself not to turn and watch as she reaches the door.

A moment later, the door shuts behind her. She's gone, leaving the director and me in silence. I force myself to stand tall as I look at him, even though I am suddenly, sickeningly aware of how easy it would be for this man to hurt me.

"You are the worst kind of fool," the director says. "You don't know what you're really asking for. You say the Nightmare is intelligent as if *that* is what we should be concerned about. As if we were only holding that creature here because we thought he was some animal to be studied." The director leans forward, stepping into my personal space. I refuse to back down, but I'm trembling. "You're right. It is not an animal, Ms. Vance. It is something much worse. It is a *monster.* A monster that has killed and would kill again. It does not matter if that thing is the best fucking philosopher of the century, because it would still be a monster. Do you understand?"

I don't, but I think I'm starting to. I stare at him, at a loss for words, as he steps back and straightens himself. His calm, unemotional mask slides back into place.

"You already knew," I say numbly. I suspected it, but I didn't want to believe that it was true. "You knew all along that he was intelligent." He must've known long before I showed up here. And yet he's continuing to treat the Nightmare like this.

"Then why?" I ask, staring up at him. "*How?* How could you do this to him?" Locking him in a cage, performing harmful experiments on him… It would be cruel for an animal. For a conscious being that rivals our own intelligence and emotional capability? It's horrible. Unthinkable.

"Because *it*," he says, straining the word, "is a monster. They are *all*"—he gestures widely to encompass the facility— "monsters."

They are all like Somnus, he is saying. They are all…conscious. Intelligent. Oh God. The implication hits me so hard, it makes me feel faintly ill. I was so focused on my own monster— my own personal quest to prove that Somnus is worthy of more than this horrible little cell—that I hadn't considered how many others in this facility might be stuck in the same way.

Or that the director and the other higher-ups already know. That they are *knowingly* keeping sentient beings trapped here, for their own sick and twisted experiments.

"We are doing the world a service by keeping that thing here, where the world does not have to fear it," he continues. "People would thank us if they knew what we were doing here. We ensure the rest of the world doesn't have to know that these goddamn freaks exist."

I knew that there was some shady stuff going down in this building. Part of me suspected that the director knew more than he let on. But never did I imagine the depths of his cruelty. I thought if I confronted him with the evidence of what he was doing, he would have no choice but to change his ways, if only to save face. But this…this is worse than I thought. He knows what he's doing, and even worse than that, he believes he is justified in it.

Dr. Wright knows too. Maybe I'm the only one working here who didn't get the memo. I could continue trying to argue, tell him that Somnus never hurt anyone until he was forced into captivity here, but I doubt it will make much of a difference to him.

Instead, it's time for Plan B.

"Well," I say, drawing myself up to my full height and pushing back my shoulders. I'm still shaky, and I certainly don't feel confident, but I hope I look it. "I guess you leave me no choice but to find out if the public agrees with that sentiment, then."

Director Ramsey goes still. It is a dangerous sort of stillness. Not like a deer in headlights, but like a predator about to strike. "Surely you're not suggesting what I think you are," he says.

"Surely you would not be *that* idiotic."

I swallow hard and push down the voice in my head that agrees with him. "That video I showed you, and the notes and other evidence I spoke of, are stored safely in a cloud database," I say, quietly and slowly so that he has no choice but to lean forward to hear me. "If I don't check in every twelve hours and input a passcode that only I know, it will be released online for the world to see. Everyone will know what's happening here."

For a moment, the director is frozen. Then a smile stretches across his face. "Oh, you really are a fool," he says. "You haven't thought this through at all, have you?"

"I *have*," I insist. "And I'm not asking for anything ridiculous. I understand the difficulties posed by releasing a being like the Nightmare into the world. I believe he should, and he will, earn more trust if we give him a chance to prove he means us no harm. For now, all I want are better conditions for him and any others who—"

The director barks out a harsh laugh and I cut off despite myself, flinching. "What do you think will happen, exactly, if that footage is released to the world?" he asks, his eyes burning into me, his face a mask of fury. "Do you think that people will be *sympathetic*?" He laughs again, grating and humorless. "No. God, no. They would be terrified. The people of Ash Valley will probably bring back the ol' torches and pitchforks. They'll tear this facility apart. Tear *us* apart, *and* that creature you're obsessed with." His smile warps. "If he doesn't tear them apart first."

I try to ignore the wriggling chill of doubt in my heart. "He wouldn't do that," I say. "The only time he hurt anyone was when he was desperate to escape."

"Even if that were true, I assure you, the other creatures here would. Gladly. Gleefully. They would slaughter this town, and then…" He holds out his hands, shaking his head. "God only knows. Maybe the military would wipe them out, or confine them. Or maybe they'd just run rampant. You really have no idea what the world was like before we could contain threats like these. You don't know how fucking good we have it!" His volume raises to a shout on the last sentence, and I'm struck into silence, standing stiff and uncertain in front of him.

"But go ahead," he continues, lowering his voice again as calm settles over his features. "Release your 'evidence.' See what the world thinks of it. Most will think it is photoshopped bullshit. They will not think it is real, because they do not want it to be. They want to carry on thinking that there are no monsters under the bed. And those who believe you…well. As I said. They will not react in the way you think." He taps his foot against the tile. *Tap-tap-tap,* like the approach of some predator. I want to flinch at every repetition as fear curls around my heart and squeezes. "And even if they are, I will ensure that *you* will not be around to enjoy it. Oh, taking you down would be almost too easy. Mr. Mayhew has told us all about your previous episodes of mental instability, your tendency to lie… We have it all in writing. I agreed to let you work here because Wright pushed for it, but I had a contingency plan ready the minute you signed your contract."

Fucking Ethan. I set my jaw, refusing to let the heat behind my eyes spill over in tears. I want to scream and rage and fight, but I know that would only make him feel more justified. I push my feelings deep down, but all that space left by my anger fills quickly with fear.

"You *and* your parents…" Director Ramsey continues. Seeing

the expression on my face, he smiles. "Yes, dear Enora and Vincent. It would be a simple thing to find them culpable in your crimes and have them meet the same fate as you."

"They have nothing to do with this," I say, the words weak even to my own ears. "You can't—"

"*Can't?*" he repeats, scathing. "That's where you're wrong again. There is very little I *can't* do to defend the security of this place, Ms. Vance. Because I, and the benefactors who keep this facility running, know exactly how important it is to maintain the secrecy we strive for. I could do anything I want to you, to your parents, to this entire fucking town, and the world would be all too eager to turn a blind eye for the sake of maintaining their status quo."

"I don't believe you." The words come out barely a whisper, not convincing even to me. "You can't just...get away with this."

The director sneers. "Go ahead," he says. "Try me."

* * *

I feel numb as the security guards escort me out. One hulking man shadows me on either side, as if I could possibly do anything to retaliate. They take my notes, of course, and my security card. I'm pushed out the door with nothing more than my cell phone—which, no doubt, has some type of tracker on it to monitor my activity—and a reminder about the lifelong NDA I signed.

I hate walking away like this. Defeated, helpless, not even given a chance to say goodbye to the Nightmare. But I have no choice, no power to exercise. I played right into the director's hands today. He's probably been waiting for an excuse to fire me, and I handed it to him.

I can't bring myself to regret what I did. Not even the heated words I spoke at the end. But I don't know how I'm going to live with the outcome. I make it halfway through my ride home before the tears start, and by the time I pull into my parents' driveway, I'm full-on sobbing. I lay my head on the steering wheel for a few moments and try to recompose myself enough to make it to my bedroom. Thankfully, my parents are still at work, so I don't run into them as I drag myself to bed. There, I lock my door, shut off the light, and curl up under the covers.

I want nothing more than to fall asleep immediately, after-noon sunlight through the window be damned, so I can see Somnus and tell him what happened. Even if I can't see him in real life, at least I still have my dreams.

But no matter how I try, I only toss and turn in bed, so tormented by my racing thoughts that I can't sink into the blissful oblivion I'm seeking. I can't stop thinking about the Nightmare being subjected to more tests, and the horrible arrogant smirk on the director's face, and his implication that the other "monsters" within the facility are much the same.

* * *

It takes a long, long time to fall asleep. But at least, when I do, Somnus is there. He holds me while I sob and explain everything to him, and murmurs reassurances as he strokes my hair.

"I'm sorry," I whisper. "I... I thought I could save you. But I screwed it all up."

"It is not your fault," he says, and presses a kiss to my forehead. "You cared enough to try, and that is more than I could have hoped for. More than anyone else has done for me."

I sniffle, pressing my cheek against his chest, breathing in the comforting smell of him. Smoke and spice, warm and masculine. Part of me is afraid that asking more will only hurt, but I have to know. "How long have you been trapped there, Somnus?"

He pauses. "I…am not sure. It is hard for me to measure time when I am so isolated."

I close my eyes, fighting back a fresh wave of grief for him. "How did you end up trapped in the first place?" I ask. I can't believe it's never come up before, but I have been so preoccupied with trying to prove his consciousness to the director that it didn't occur to me to ask.

"Hmm…" He shifts, and for a moment I'm afraid he's going to pull away. But instead, he settles into a more comfortable position, cradling me against his chest with one large arm. "It started when I fell in love."

My breath hitches.

"Most of my kind exist almost entirely in the realm of dreams. Our physical forms are naught but shadows, drifting from place to place, finding new humans to attach to. We're vulnerable in the waking world, so we stay hidden. And at night we follow our humans into dreams, where we take whatever form we believe will frighten them. That fear feeds us, makes us more powerful.

"But then… I met a woman who was not afraid of me. She was a lucid dreamer, and had almost as much control over the sleep realm as I did. It intrigued me. I had never seen a human as anything more than prey. I found myself drifting back to her dreams, again and again…and the more I learned about her, the more I tried to shape myself in a form that would please her. I found myself becoming more and more human. My kind scoffed at me, shunned me, but I told myself it was fine so long as I had her. And then…then I made the mistake of going to her in my physical form."

He sighs and is silent for several long seconds. I wrap my arms more tightly around him and wait until he is ready to continue.

"I thought we had formed a bond. I thought that if I approached her in a human form, she would accept me. But though she did not fear me in her dreams, she was terrified when she saw me in the waking world. Still, I lingered, hoping to fix things between us, but…" He shakes his head. "She betrayed me. Led me out into the light of day, where I was weakest, and then had me captured by agents of the research center where you now work. I have been trapped since, but for one brief escape, many years ago." He closes his eyes. "For a very long time, I thought it was my fault. I had tried to be human and I had failed. I was a monster, like they said."

For a moment I just hold him, trying to comfort him as he has been comforting me. "I'm sorry that happened to you," I finally say, and swallow. "I'm sorry she didn't understand you. I know what it's like to fall for the wrong person. To place your trust in someone who doesn't deserve it. But I hope you know it wasn't your fault, what happened." I look up at him, paraphrasing words my therapist once told me. "It takes courage to be vulnerable. And to do that—to open your heart to someone—is the most human thing there is."

He slowly opens his eyes and smiles down at me. Even with his sharp teeth, it somehow comes off soft. "I am glad to have met you, Samara Vance," he says.

"Me too." I drape a leg over him and cuddle closer against his warmth. "At least we have this. They can never really separate us when we have our dreams."

Somnus hesitates, and I almost think he's going to say something. But then he leans down and kisses me, and as we fall back on the bed, I soon forget the moment.

Chapter Twenty-One

The next week passes sluggishly. During the day, I feel like a zombie, shuffling around the house and barely aware of what I'm doing. I probably wouldn't even remember to eat, if not for my concerned parents' reminders. They insist on eating dinner together every night, even though I'm terrible company as I sit and mope and push food around my plate. I know they're doing their best to help—comforting me about the loss of my job, gently urging me to leave the house, never asking questions I'm not ready to answer—but nothing breaks through my depressed haze.

Nights are my only escape. I spend all of my waking hours looking forward to the moment I get to crawl into bed and fall asleep. At first, I tuck in early, even before my parents do, but all that gets me is hours of tossing and turning and struggling to quiet my mind enough to actually drift off. After a few days of that torture, I turn to other means. First I rummage through my parents' cabinet for Nyquil, but that renders my dreams murky and strange, not as clear and *real* as they usually are with Somnus. I think of going to the doctor and begging for a prescription sleep aid, but I worry that would have much of the same effect. So I settle for ordering some melatonin and start running every evening at sundown. I push myself to the point of exhaustion, so that by the time my head hits the pillow there is nothing my aching body can do *other* than sleep.

I am dimly aware that I am on the path to destroying myself. This is no way to live. But dreams are the only thing in my life that make me happy right now. My dreams, and the Nightmare waiting for me in them.

It is bittersweet, to be cut off from Somnus in real life but always find him waiting after I close my eyes. I do my best to enjoy this time together because it is all we have. Sometimes our nights are wild and indulgent, leaving me rumpled and breathless and pleasantly sore when I awake. Other times we just lie together, his huge body curled around mine, his claws stroking my hair and his low rumble of a voice in my ear.

As time goes on, I let myself start to believe that this is enough for me. Even if I am cut off from the Facility, so long as Somnus is there when I fall into bed at night, maybe I will be okay. Bit by bit, that thought helps me drag myself from the dark pit of my depression. I start searching for jobs online, thinking about my future again, considering moving back to the city. I'm surprisingly sad when I think of leaving Ash Valley now. Not just because of the Nightmare, but also due to the new friends I found in Ezra and Belle, and the peaceful nostalgia of Cup o' Happy, and dinners with my parents. Once, I was so eager to leave, but I feel as though coming back here with fresh eyes made me realize how much I truly loved it.

I always vowed that I wouldn't settle down here, wouldn't end up sucked into the "black hole" of the town like so many others. Now I'm starting to realize maybe that's because people don't realize how good they had it here until they leave…but oh well. I try to convince myself that this will be a good thing for me. A fresh start, away from the open wound that the Facility has become, and all of the secrets I am probably better off not knowing.

And no matter where I go, I will have Somnus. I will always carry a piece of home with me, wherever I go. I will always have my dreams with him.

Or so I think. Until one day, I reach for him and my hand goes through his arm.

I blink. Reach again. This time I manage to grip him, but he still feels less substantial, his form colder, less firm. I look up to meet his eyes. His expression is troubled...and not surprised. Once I look closer, I see that he is changing, too. His form has grown hazy around the edges, his features less distinct than usual. It's the same with the recreation of my room, the whole dream. Everything feels dimmer, further from reality. As though it is a normal dream, rather than the special dream space we usually enjoy together.

My heart sinks. "What's happening?" I ask. "Are you okay?"

He sighs and pulls me closer. I nestle into his lap and try to reassure myself that he is still here. "I am all right," he says, stroking my hair. But even his fingers running through my waves feels different, like a rustle of a breeze, rather than solid fingers. I shut my eyes tightly, trying to focus on the sensation as if that will anchor him here. "It is...our bond. It is fading."

My eyes snap open. "What?" I ask.

"I require a physical closeness to make my way into someone's dreams," he explains. "When I was able to see you every day, even for a few hours, it was more than enough. An easy thing to follow you into your dreams. But now...it is getting harder to find you. Harder to maintain this space for us."

No. Dr. Wright did mention something about that once, but

I let it slip my mind. Maybe I was eager to forget. I stare up at Somnus, tears welling in my eyes. It feels so unfair. Even after everything that's happened, I thought at least we could have these moments together. But Director Ramsey has stolen even my dreams from me. "Why didn't you tell me?"

Guilt is etched on his shadowed features. "I was not sure how. I thought we would have more time. But I am also…in a weakened state."

"Weakened how?" I pull back and look at him more sharply. "Are they hurting you?" He looks away, and I can sense that he's about to try to dodge the question. I grab him by the chin and force him to look at me. "Look at me! Tell me the truth."

He chuckles at my boldness, but when he meets my eyes as requested, there is pain and sorrow in those black depths. "I am being kept isolated. It…cuts me off from the dream world. I have no dreams of my own. I need to latch on to those of others."

Despair wells up within me; it feels like something is breaking into jagged shards deep in my chest. "So you…you will be all alone in that tiny cell."

"It is not the first time," he says. "There have been periods when I have been isolated for a long, long while."

I think back to when I first glimpsed him in that room—his amorphous shape, his sluggish movements—and how eagerly he responded when he heard a human voice, saw a human face.

How he slowly changed into a more humanoid form again. A suspicion nags at me, so horrible I am tempted to push it away before I can confirm it, but I can't let myself. "You were alone for a while before I began to work there, weren't you?" I ask quietly.

He looks at me. Dips his head in a barely perceptible nod. "How long, Somnus?"

He sighs, a sound like the wind rustling through leaves. "I am not sure," he says. "A very long time. I was being punished. I acted out in anger, tried to escape."

I stare at him, swallowing hard. "They told me your escape attempt was in the eighties. That was…that was *decades* ago."

His silence speaks for itself.

I curl my shaking hands into fists. I will not let them do that to him again. Will not let them lock him in that cell until he forgets what a human face looks like.

"No," I say stubbornly. "No. I refuse. I'm not going to let this happen."

His claws ghost over my face, no more substantial than the wind. His expression is deeply sad. "There is nothing you can do, Mara. Do not get yourself hurt for my sake. I will survive. I always have."

I reach for him, desperate, but my hands go straight through him. It's like trying to cling to smoke. He's fading even more, in front of my very eyes. Disappearing. I catch a glimpse of dawn peeking through the window and know with a horrible lurch of my stomach that this will be our last dream together.

"Wait," I say. "No, please, wait. Tell me what to do. Tell me how I can find you again!"

The Nightmare shakes his head. His lips form a word, but I can't hear it. Everything is fading: his face, his voice, the room. My mind is trying to wake up, but I cling as hard as I can.

"Please," I say. "Somnus—"

I wake up, alone, with sunlight streaming through the window.

Chapter Twenty-Two

For the next couple of hours, all I can do is lie in bed and stare at the ceiling. Depression sinks into my bones—but I fight it off with a wave of anger.

This situation is so goddamn unfair. But most of all, right now, I'm angry at myself. I was so eager to accept my own helplessness. So ready to walk away from this, find some new job in some new city, and forget about everything. Too content to have Somnus visit in my dreams and ignore the fact that he's suffering in the real world. But now I realize how wrong I was. Even if he hadn't been ripped from my dreams as well, it would have been horribly selfish of me to think that situation was acceptable.

The thought of being parted from Somnus forever, including in my dreams, is agony. But even worse is the idea of him being trapped there. Alone. Experimented on by people who don't care about him, who don't understand him or make any effort to do so. Director Ramsey is hurting him, and he doesn't care. The sick fuck probably enjoys it. And whoever ends up with my old job may not even realize what they're really doing there. Even if they do, they might not care. They might look at Somnus and see only the monster that the director wants them to see.

I can't leave him there. The thought terrifies me when it first occurs to me, but it also feels *right*. I will not abandon him. Not now and not ever. He deserves better than a life of captivity and torment.

Whatever it takes, I'm going to break my monster out of his cage.

* * *

I don't have a lot of allies, but I do have a couple, or so I hope. So, after careful consideration and planning, I invite Belle and Ezra out to dinner again. I consider reaching out to Dr. Wright but ultimately decide against it. For a minute I believed she was on my side, but the risk is too great, and she's lied to me too many times. I believe she has a different endgame than Director Ramsey does, but I don't think that necessarily means she's my ally.

Of course, I don't know if Belle and Ezra will be either. But I know that they're good people, and the closest thing to friends I have in this town. I also know that I can't pull this off alone. So I have to try.

I shower and dress with the grim determination of a soldier preparing for battle. Even though I feel like wallowing in my days-old sweatpants with dried tears on my face, I can't. I won't. I need to build some momentum so that I don't fall into that yawning abyss of helplessness again. I also need to make sure that Belle and Ezra will take me seriously rather than viewing me as a jaded, spiteful, possibly unhinged ex-coworker.

It feels weird to have this conversation in public, but I'm more worried about my house being bugged than I am about locals overhearing us, so we meet at the diner again. When they arrive, we settle into the same booth we did last time, tucked away in a corner of the mostly empty restaurant. The vibe is a little awkward, since they're both doubtlessly aware of the fact that I've been fired, but they still showed up. That has to mean something.

I take a deep breath and lean back in my seat, the plastic booth crinkling beneath me. "Okay," I say. "I need to tell you something, and it's going to sound fucking crazy, but please hear me out before you pass any judgments."

Belle nods so quickly that my heart melts. Ezra takes a second longer, but he nods too.

I pour it all out: my experiences with Somnus, and my growing conviction that he's more intelligent and closer to human than the higher-ups led me to believe. My refusal to continue torturing him, and how it ended up getting me fired. And, lastly, my determination to get him out of there.

It takes a long time. And when I'm done, silence is thick in the air.

"And there's one more thing." I wasn't sure about doing this, but now that I'm here, I feel like I need to prove myself. I fumble in my pocket and pull out my phone. Director Ramsey destroyed the burner phone I snuck into the facility, but I still have the cloud files. And while doing this could undoubtedly put me in even more danger, at this point, I'm all in. "I have proof. Videos. Here." I pull up a clip. It's not one of the ones I used to try to prove his intelligence, but one of the bloopers in between our more serious conversations: me attempting shadow puppetry while he tries to match the shape of my hands. Me, laughing brightly, while his own shoulders shake in silent amusement. Our hands pressing against opposite sides of the glass in a farewell.

As it ends, I'm left feeling exposed. There's no mistaking the tenderness I feel for Somnus in this clip. It takes me a few seconds to work up the courage to glance at the others. Ezra has a hand over his mouth and an unreadable expression. Belle is as pale as a sheet. At first, I think she's afraid of what I'm proposing, and my stomach sinks; maybe it was a mistake, inviting her here.

But after a moment, Belle whispers, "I thought I was imagining things." She raises her eyes to meet mine, and I can see how shaken she is. "But my subject is the same way. I'm not allowed to interact with her—it—" She shakes her head, grimacing in frustration. "No, *her*. I'm not allowed to interact with her directly, but I can tell from my observations. She's smarter than they say she is. She doesn't deserve to be trapped there in a tank." Her voice grows as she continues, and by the end of it the color is back in her cheeks and her eyes are bright. Then she pauses, and her lower lip trembles slightly. "She doesn't deserve any of the things they do to her."

Something about the look on her face makes me wonder if her bond with her subject is a little more than platonic, like mine is.

I'm ashamed to admit I didn't consider the other subjects in the Facility, even after I began to suspect that many of them are the same as my Nightmare. But now I find myself wondering how deep this goes. That building is huge, probably lined with cells... Who knows how many of them are intelligent beings, held against their will? Trapped by the belief that they're dangerous? Maybe some of them are deadly like the director says…but I'd be willing to bet that others are just different, just misunderstood, like Somnus.

Either way, the determination on Belle's face tells me that I have an ally in her. I look over at Ezra, who is still sitting with a hand over his mouth and a wrinkled, worried expression.

"I haven't been able to observe any of the subjects closely," he says slowly. "My work takes me all around the Facility, so I get only glimpses. Yet I have to admit I've seen…things…that have made me doubt the morality of what we're doing." He swallows hard. I want to press harder, hear more about what he's experienced and what he might know about the nature of the Facility, but the guilt already etched in his expression stops me. "I believe… I have *always* believed…that just because something is different doesn't make it bad." As he pauses, the light reflects off his eyes, and I swear I catch a flash of something strange and shimmering in them—but then he blinks, and the moment passes. "But some of them *are* dangerous. I've seen the evidence of that too." He turns a scrutinizing gaze on me. "Are you sure it will be safe to set X-13 free?"

I want to blurt out a yes, but I force myself to pause. To think. I need to weigh this decision carefully. I have been fooled before, by monsters like Ethan who look like men— fooled so thoroughly that I began to doubt my own mind. I am not ashamed of being manipulated, but I am determined not to let it happen to me ever again.

I go over everything I've experienced with the Nightmare, everything I've learned from my interactions with him. But, especially when I compare him to my experience with Ethan, the answer is clear. Ethan was always a perfect golden boy in public, and horribly cruel to me when we were alone. Somnus is, in a way, the inverse—the world views him as a monster, but privately, he has shown me that he is gentle and understanding and kind.

"Yes," I say finally. "I trust him. He has never hurt me, and never hurt anyone at all until he was trapped against his will. If he's free, he won't harm anyone. You have my word."

"And you're ready to take responsibility for him?" Ezra asks, holding my gaze. His expression is not harsh or doubting, but it is very, very serious.

I don't look away or hesitate for a second. "Yes," I say. "I am."

He takes a deep breath and then gives a slow, decisive nod. "Okay," he says. "In that case, I have an idea about how we could make this work."

Chapter Twenty-Three

It turns out those "crazy" rumors were right. It *is* possible to listen in on the Facility chatter via radio if you're close enough. I lurk around the back of the building, ear pressed to a handheld device, listening to bits and pieces of crackling voices interspersed by static. Ezra snuck me through the gate this morning, and now I'm waiting for the signal for part two of our plan.

I don't have to wait long.

"Security breach." I'm surprised how good of an actress Belle is; she sounds shaken and breathless over the radio. "Subject X-12 has escaped from its tank."

For a moment, there's nothing. Then the gruff, half-familiar voice of a security guard says, "Please repeat?"

"X-12, designation *the Siren*, has escaped from its tank," Belle says again, more firmly, though her voice still trembles. "Dr. Langley is injured. I need help evacuating him."

Anxiety spikes through me. An injury was not part of the plan, so maybe this isn't Belle's acting at all but genuine panic. Either way, what follows is exactly as predicted: a flurry of chaos. The radio is flooded with questions and alarmed shouts, until the security guard yells at everybody to keep the channel clear for orders.

"Initiating full lockdown, code red," he says, a moment after everyone else goes quiet. "All personnel evacuate the facility immediately. Sending two units to assist with Dr. Langley."

I shut the radio off, clutch it to my chest, and press myself against the side of the building beside a dumpster marked with biohazard symbols. My heart is hammering in my ears and my body trembling with adrenaline, but all I can do right now is wait. I didn't even bring my cell phone today, just in case it's being tracked, so I have no way of contacting the others if things go awry.

Soon, I hear the metal screech of the back door opening. I stay where I am as footsteps approach, afraid it will be a stranger fleeing the building, but Ezra peeks around the corner and gestures at me.

"Seems that things have gone a bit off the rails already," he says. His teeth worry at his lower lip.

"How far off the rails?"

"The Siren took a chunk out of a doctor's arm the second she was out of the tank."

"Oh," I say. I lose my nerve for a second, thinking of some vicious creature loose in the facility halls. But then I remember what Belle said the other night, her obvious dismay over the Siren's treatment here. "Think he deserved it?" I blurt out before I can stop myself.

Ezra stares at me for a moment and then breaks into a shaky smile. "You know," he says, digging his security card out of his pocket, "from what I've seen, yeah, he did." He presses the card into my palm but holds on as I reach for it. "Be careful," he says, holding my gaze meaningfully before he lets go.

I nod, clinging to the security card like a lifeline. "I will.

Thank you."

He jogs away to join the other evacuated employees, and I head for the back door. I scan his security card, and just like that, I'm inside.

The plan was to cause enough chaos to allow me to slip in unnoticed and find Somnus. While things haven't gone exactly as intended, we do have a damn good distraction.

I've never used the back entrance before, and the Facility feels surreal and alien, especially with the blood-red emergency lights flashing on every corner. An alarm wails somewhere, high-pitched like a woman screaming. I hurry my steps through the empty halls and listen for footsteps indicating security or other personnel approaching, but the place is eerily empty, just an endless hallway of locked metal doors. I'm itching to see what's behind them—and I have a feeling Ezra's security card could open at least a few—but I stay focused on my goal. There isn't much time until someone realizes what's going on, and I have to be long gone with the Nightmare by then.

Two left turns and one right later, I find the control room, right where Ezra told me I would when we first formulated the plan. Part of me is nervous that the door won't open due to the lockdown, but that fear proves unfounded, and soon I slip inside.

The control room is cramped, boxy, and thankfully empty. Pale fluorescent lighting makes the whole place look washed-out and surreal. One wall is entirely taken up with screens displaying various security feeds. There's a desk with a few computer monitors, along with a radio emitting a stream of staticky chatter, and a still-steaming mug of coffee that must have been left behind by somebody fleeing the building.

I stare up at the cameras. My breath catches in my throat. So long I've imagined this moment, wished I knew more, and now, here it is: the Facility and its menagerie of monsters.

I catch a glimpse of a green-tinged man covered in stitches and tattoos, a room that looks empty except for the objects being hurled around violently, and a winged creature so bright that it hurts to look at it for more than a second.A monster with a snake's body and a man's head, and another that looks like a woman made of fire.

There's also a tall woman with long, wet hair, completely naked and covered in shimmering scales, wandering through the empty hallways with blood on her hands and face. There's no sound from the video feed, but her lips move like she's speaking...or singing.

I remember Belle's words on the radio. *X-12...the Siren.* I have to hope I won't run into her, or that if I do, Belle was right when she said she could be reasoned with. I tear my eyes away from her and continue looking through the video feeds.

There are so many creatures locked in this facility...but I feel sad, instead of frightened of them.

But what *does* scare me is that I can't find Somnus among them.

I look over the screens one by one, but I catch no glimpse of my familiar shadowed figure. Finally, I realize that there's no footage at all for cell 13; they must have shut the cameras off. I'm afraid to think of what that might mean.

But no matter what undoubtedly horrible things the director has put him through, I'm here now to save him.

Judging by the camera feeds, security hasn't entered the building yet, but I know it's only a matter of time until they pull together an effort to recapture the Siren. There's no time to delay. I search through the control panels until I find the switch for cell 13 and swap it to the *unlocked* position. Electricity jolts through me as I do so, a delicious thrill and sense of satisfaction.

The Nightmare is free. Now all that's left is to go claim him.

Chapter Twenty-Four

I probably look insane, a recently fired employee sprinting through the building with a wild grin on my face. I can imagine them running video clips of this during news segments, *unstable ex-employee stages dangerous jail break*, et cetera, but I can't bring myself to care right now. The only thing at the forefront of my mind is the Nightmare. Somnus is waiting for me. This will be not only a reunion, but a first meeting of sorts. I am so excited to see him, touch him, hold and be held by him.

I run past the door to my usual observation workspace, and instead go the next door over: room 13B, the cell I usually observe. When I pull on the handle, the metal creaks open and reveals the room I've only seen from the other side of a window.

Then the smell hits me. It is rank and animal. Like a filthy, damp dog.

I go still. This is not the smoke and spice of my Nightmare. My instincts scream *wrong*, scream *run*, and I realize that I've made a mistake a moment before I hear the wet snuffle of something in the corner.

This cell is occupied, but not by Somnus.

Slowly, I turn to face the creature lurking in the shadows of the room. It stands at least eight feet tall, and is as thick as a tree. It's bipedal and covered in matted brown fur, with a pair of twin horns curving out of its head. Each limb bulges with muscle in a way that is nearly obscene, and it is clad only in a filthy-looking loincloth. For a moment I can only stare, but then my brain catches up and supplies a name for what I'm looking at: *minotaur*.

There doesn't seem to be any intelligence in its beady black eyes. But I was wrong with the Nightmare at first. Maybe I'm wrong now too.

"Hello…" I try, my voice coming out thin and weak. I take a step back, and it growls, so I freeze again. "Can you…speak? Or understand me?" I ask, but my heart is already sinking as I observe the way it's looking at me, its lack of a reaction to my attempts to speak to it, other than a flick of its tapered ears.

It takes a step toward me. A cloven hoof scrapes at the tile. I take a step back, suppressing the urge to run. I know what they say about turning your back to a predator, and this thing definitely feels like one.

"Okay, okay… Sorry for intruding…" I babble, attempting a soothing voice that comes out too high-pitched with anxiety. My body quakes as I slowly back toward the door. *Just a couple more steps, a couple more.*

Then the Minotaur lets out an angry snort. It stamps one hoof on the ground, and I'm hit with a distinct flashback to a viral video featuring a bull about to charge.

I turn and bolt out the door, flinging it half shut behind me. Not a second later, there's a deep bellow and an earth-shattering crash as the Minotaur slams into it. Metal screeches horribly. I glance over my shoulder, still running, to see that the creature has ripped the door off its hinges and flung it to the floor. Now it's in the hallway, and its beady eyes are still locked on me, filled with rage.

"Shit, shit, shit," I whisper. I ran in a panic, and now, I realize with a lurch, I'm heading deeper into the Facility, toward endless locked doors and God knows what else rather than outside where the guards can defend me. But it's too late to turn back; the Minotaur is prowling after me, its bulky form filling most of the hallway. All I can do is keep running.

The melancholic wail of the alarm is still going off somewhere in the building. Between its screams, I can hear another, distant noise. Is someone…singing? But no time to focus on that. The monster behind me bellows again, as though the sounds have further enraged it. *Just what I fucking need right now.* I'm distantly aware that my plan is falling apart. Any chance of stealth or secrecy is fully gone. I have to focus on getting out alive. The rest can wait until I'm *not* being chased by an eight-foot-tall bull monster who could snap my spine with one hand.

God, I wish I had my own monster at my side right now. I didn't have a plan to get *out* of here once I was inside—I figured with Somnus, we could figure it out together. And even while I'm running desperately for my life, I can't help but worry about him. Where is he? What have they done with him?

I swipe Ezra's card at door after door between bouts of sprinting to get ahead of the minotaur, but none of them open. When I pound on a few in desperation, there's no answer. My breath becomes ragged, my legs shaky with exhaustion and panic as I navigate a seemingly never-ending spiral of hallways, deeper and deeper into the facility. And every minute, the minotaur is getting closer. I can hear its heavy, plodding steps following me, its horrible grunting and snuffling. It follows me slowly but steadily, like it has all the time in the world. And it probably does. I have nowhere to go; sooner or later, I'm going to hit a dead end, and then I'm done for.

Soon my breath leaves in gasping sobs, and I'm stumbling rather than sprinting. I have yet to see another soul. The building has fully evacuated. Is security coming? Or is it just me and this goddamn monster in an empty building of locked doors? The thought makes me want to collapse in a heap.

Just when I think I can't take it anymore, I round a corner and plow into someone. We both go sprawling onto the floor.

"Help me, please—" I gasp, before realizing who's under me.

Dr. Calliope Wright stares up at me with a look of equal parts bewilderment and anger. "You," she says, somehow managing to sound shaken and furious at the same time. "What have you done?"

As if in response, the minotaur bellows behind me, the deep sound reverberating through the hallway. It's close. Terrifyingly close. I scramble to my feet and reach down to help Dr. Wright up as well. No matter what's happened between us, I'm not going to leave her to the mercy of that *thing*.

Her face is still calm, but her eyes are wide as she accepts my hand. Once she's on her feet, she immediately kicks off her heels in preparation to run. "How many of them have you let out?" she asks, only the slightest tremble betraying her fear as the clomping hooves come closer.

"Just the one," I say, still struggling to catch my breath. "The Minotaur."

"Fuck," she says succinctly. "Come with me."

She takes off. I hesitate for only a moment. I'm not sure I

can trust her, but I'm *damn* sure the creature behind me will rip me apart given half the chance. So I sprint after Dr. Wright, forcing my already tired body to go a little further.

When I reach the end of the hallway, she's opening one of the endless doors with her security card. As she steps in and looks back, for one horrifying moment I think she's going to slam it shut and leave me out here alone. Instead, she holds the door open and impatiently waves me in. I stumble past her and sink to the tile in relief, my breath coming in short, panicky bursts.

I try to ground myself by taking in my surroundings. We're now locked in a tiny, nondescript office. A metal desk, two chairs, and a clunky, old-school computer in a square room with the same white walls and white tile as the rest of the building.

Dr. Wright shuts and locks the door behind us, and then goes to an intercom on the wall and hits a button. "This is Dr. Wright," she says. "Still trapped within the building, and we have another security breach. Subject X-9, the Minotaur, last seen approaching my office."

Just as she finishes, there's a heavy *thunk* against the door. Our heads whip toward it, and I see that the metal is dented.

Dr. Wright swallows and says, in the same terse voice, "X-9 is now just outside my office door."

She hangs up the intercom, grabs one of the metal chairs from her desk, and wedges it under the door handle. The Minotaur slams against the door again, and she stumbles back, sucking in a breath.

"It just had to be that one," she mutters.

I scuttle back against the wall and sit there, wrapping my arms around my knees. "Can it be reasoned with?" I ask, though I fear I know the answer.

She sighs. "Absolutely not," she says wearily. "It's one of the few that can't be."

I bite my lip. I want to ask more, and to find a way to get to Somnus. But right now, I have to worry about my own safety. "What do we do?"

"Hide until the security team takes care of it," she says. But then she walks over and tucks herself underneath her metal desk, which is not exactly reassuring.

If I stay here and wait for security, I'm screwed. Somnus will be stuck here, and I'll end up in prison for everything I did today. But what choice do I have? The only way out of here is blocked by a creature that wants to kill us.

The thing slams against the door again. The hinges creak with the strain. I bite back a scream and shut my eyes, wishing again that Somnus were here. If the minotaur gets into this room, we're fucked. There is no way to escape from here. A dead end.

But a few moments later, I perk up at the muffled sound of gunfire from outside and a roar from the monster, even louder than the bursts of automatic weaponry. The slamming against the door stops. There's more firing, more bellowing, and then…

Silence.

I look toward Dr. Wright, who is still hiding beneath her desk.

Part of me agrees with the sentiment. But even if something has gone wrong with the security team, even if they haven't managed to take the minotaur down, it's possible they managed to lead it elsewhere and give us a chance to escape. We can't just hide here forever.

"Should we look outside?" I whisper.

For a moment I think she's just going to keep hiding. But a moment later, Dr. Wright slowly emerges, moving at a crouch toward the doorway. "Keep your mouth shut," she whispers at me. I nod but sidle up to the door alongside her, desperate for a look myself.

She nudges the chair to the side and eases the dented door open a crack. She peers out.

I catch only slivers of the scene outside: blood splattered across the walls. A still-twitching limb. A spill of guts across the tile.

And somewhere around the bend of the hallway, out of sight, is the horrible, wet sound of chewing between heavy, snorting breaths.

Dr. Wright eases the door shut again. She stands up and presses her back to it, and we stare at each other. Her gaze is as haunted and hunted as I feel.

"What do we do?" I ask, my voice trembling.

She shakes her head. Her calm mask, always in place, is starting to crack, and that scares me more than anything.

"Do you have a weapon in here? Or another way out?" I ask.

She lets out a small, hollow laugh in response.

I bite my lip. "Okay, okay… Well… It's distracted, at least," I say, trying to think through the haze of panic over my thoughts. "It knows we're in here, so we should move while we can. Is there somewhere else we can go? Somewhere safer?" I consider the question myself. "Can we get to the control room, and out the back door?"

Dr. Wright scrubs a hand over her face and regains a hint of her composure. "Yes," she says. "I have clearance." Then her expression crumples. "If we can make it. That thing… It cut through the security team in minutes, it…"

"This is our only shot," I say, before she can spiral. "We have to take it. It's that or sit here and wait to die."

She swallows, nods curtly. "Yes. You're right." She brushes a trembling hand over the front of her silk shirt. "Let's go, then."

After a moment's hesitation, I hold out a hand. She stares at it for a moment and then reaches over and tangles her fingers with mine. Her other hand reaches for the door handle. She holds my gaze and mouths: *Three... two... one,* and opens the door. I grimace at the creak of metal, and we peer through the crack into the hallway outside.

There is nothing moving out there. Only bright splashes of blood—and bodies, strewn in pieces. I swallow back bile and follow as Dr. Wright slips through the door. I ease it shut behind us, and we both stand with our backs pressed to it, staring at the scene in front of us.

I must be going into shock, because I feel numb as I look around, taking in the terrible sights in bits and pieces. A dismembered arm with teeth marks. Blank staring eyes, open mouths, a radio still crackling with static. The hallway is quiet otherwise…but not silent. I can hear a sound from around the corner. An animalistic snuffling, followed by a wet tear and horrible chewing.

My stomach lurches. But Dr. Wright grips my hand and tugs me forward. I follow, taking an effort not to step on any of the body parts. This is all my fault, I realize. I freed the monster that did this. Yet I can't bring myself to feel guilty. Maybe that will come later, but right now, I feel angry. And I cannot help but tell myself that I am not really to blame.

It doesn't feel like a coincidence that the director moved the Nightmare from his usual room, the room he knew I would go to, and placed such a dangerous creature inside. Maybe he didn't anticipate this exact scenario happening, but I suspect he knew I would try to do something. I'm sure he hoped it would be me that ended up being torn to pieces and snacked on. Part of me spitefully thinks it'll grate on him to know that he got his own men killed instead…but given what I know of the director, I doubt he'll care.

Dr. Wright and I sneak as quietly as we can down the hallway, and further into the building. It feels like I'm backing myself into a corner, going farther from the entrance, but I have no choice but to place my trust in Calliope now. We're in this together. And I'm especially glad for it as we reach a door that requires a passcode.

I keep an eye on the hallway behind us. It's only when I strain to listen that I realize the horrible munching sounds of the Minotaur have gone silent. Instead, it's replaced with an even worse sound: the slow clop of its hooves, coming this way.

And coming from another branch of the hallway: the sound of singing, growing louder.

"Dr. Wright," I whisper, the word barely more than a breath. My eyes twitch between the corners of the two hallways, dread billowing in my stomach.

"Not now," she mutters, inputting a password one slow number at a time, her movements precise and careful.

"Calliope—"

Her hand goes still as one gigantic hoof rounds the corner. It is followed by a hairy leg, thick with muscle, then the matted and gore-stained torso, and finally, that horrible face. Its nose twitches, and its beady eyes fix on us.

"Shit, shit, shit," I chant under my breath, my voice going

thin and reedy. I glance at Dr. Wright, who refuses to look at the Minotaur as she continues inputting a ridiculously long passcode. Finally, she finishes, and swipes her security card. The machine lets out a sharp beep.

But it doesn't sound like the good kind of beep. It sounds like a wrong answer. And a quick glance at Dr. Wright's face shows pure shock written across her face.

"What—" She breathes, and then, softer, "that *fucker*."

The Minotaur huffs out a breath and scrapes one hoof against the tile.

I tug on Dr. Wright's hand and sprint away, further down the hallway and toward the sound of singing.

Chapter Twenty-Five

I round the corner and skid to a stop at the sight of an approaching figure. Dr. Wright comes to a halt behind me, swears, and begins to back away, only to stop as the Minotaur's clopping hooves round the corner behind us. The creature stops and scents the air, seeming confused. But Dr. Wright and I are far from safe, trapped between one monster and another.

Ahead of us is the Siren. She's stopped singing, and instead, regards us with wide-set eyes, her pupils slit like a reptile's and her gaze flat. Even after catching a glimpse of her on a video feed, she is still a shocking sight, at least six feet tall, covered in metallic silver-blue scales that shine and shift as she moves. Her fingers and bare toes are joined with thin webbing, but aside from that and the scales, she looks mostly human. Yet still, there is an unearthly quality to her beautiful face; it is a little too symmetrical, her features a little too far apart, giving her an alien allure that is somehow both magnetizing and frightening.

I once heard a theory that the existence of the uncanny valley implies that humans once had reason to fear creatures that look almost, but not *quite*, like them. Looking at the Siren now, my gut screams that this is it. This is the reason. Especially with blood smeared across her full lips and dripping from her clawed hands.

But the fur-matted, blood-drenched Minotaur behind us is no better. I have the feeling that either of these creatures easily could and gladly would rip us to shreds.

Part of my mind screams for me to just drop to the tile, go into the fetal position, and pray for mercy. But it's the same part of my brain that told me to fear the Nightmare's claws and sharp teeth—an instinct that isn't always right. My heart whispers otherwise, and I have to trust it.

I set my shoulders, take a deep breath, and look at the Siren. She looks at me with her too-far-apart eyes and beautiful, expressionless face.

"We're friends of Belle," I say. No reaction. I swallow and try again. "Belle, the tech who helped free you."

"I know who Belle is, human," she says in a sweet, musical voice.

I force a wavery smile. "See? So we have a mutual friend."

She regards me, unimpressed. Behind me, I hear the shuffling sound of the Minotaur moving forward. Dr. Wright presses up against my back, her breath hitching.

"I'm here to save my own research subject," I say, the words rushing out of me without time to think about them. "X-13. The Nightmare." I swallow, fear making my head swim. "He's in danger, and I have to go to him. Because I... I love him." Out of the corner of my eye, I see Dr. Wright's head jerk toward me in surprise, but I keep my gaze fixed on the Siren. "So please, let us pass."

Once I'm done, the silence rings in my ears. The Siren's striking, cold face does not show a hint of a reaction.

Behind us, the Minotaur roars and charges. I scream, throwing myself to the floor with Dr. Wright beside me.

Then the Siren's mouth opens, and song pours out. All around us, the world seems to slow to a stop.

All at once my fear is gone, replaced by a pleasant haze. There is no bellowing minotaur or screaming alarm, just the music coming from the Siren's mouth. The song is wordless, but if I listen hard, I almost feel like I can decipher some meaning in it. I stare reverently up at the Siren as she steps toward me. I want her to touch me, to hold me, to look into my eyes and keep singing to me forever and ever.

I reach for her as she approaches, fingers brushing against the scales of her legs, and am distantly aware of Dr. Wright doing the same, her face blank like she's sleepwalking. But the Siren steps past us, toward the Minotaur, who is as frozen as we are. His beady eyes are fixed on her. She stops in front of the creature and reaches up to caress its hairy face.

Then the Siren's mouth closes, and the song stops. I blink, confused before realization and fresh terror wash over me. I crawl away from the two monsters on my hands and knees. Beside me on the floor, Dr. Wright shakes off the same trance with a shuddery breath.

The Minotaur, too, sheds its momentary placidness. Its eyes fill with rage, and its ears go flat against its head. But before it can move, the Siren shifts her hand to rest around its thick neck and snaps it in one clean motion.

She steps aside with effortless grace as its huge body thuds to the floor. Dr. Wright and I stay on the floor, staring, as the Siren slowly turns to look back at us.

She smiles, revealing a mouth lined with multiple layers of sharp teeth, like a shark.

"Run, humans," she says.

Dr. Wright and I both scramble to our feet and obey, sprinting down the hallway deeper into the Facility.

My mind is too full of animal fear to form coherent thoughts, but eventually Dr. Wright yanks me to a stop. She tries to swipe her keycard with trembling hands, but it rejects it, again and again. Finally, I grab Ezra's from my pocket, and it lets us through.

She runs inside, and I fling myself in after her, breathing hard. We're back in the abandoned control room, with the many screens and extensive control panel. As the door shuts behind us, she sinks into a metal chair. I stumble against the wall, a hand clutching my chest and the racing heart within.

"Holy fucking shit," I say.

"Agreed," Dr. Wright says. Her voice is steady, but her hands tremble as she raises them and runs them through her hair. "We made it." She takes a couple of deep breaths and then pulls herself up tall. "Now we can exit through the back and—"

"No," I say vehemently. "First, we free the Nightmare."

She blinks at me, eyebrows rising before her expression returns to its usual, calm state. "Are you out of your mind?" she asks.

"No." I gulp down more air, trying to collect myself enough to form coherent thoughts. "I meant what I said back there. I... I care about him. I'm not leaving without him." Now that I'm physically safe, my anxiety for him rushes back. "He wasn't in his cell. Where is he?"

Dr. Wright looks at me wearily. "Director Ramsey has him," she says. She hesitates and then clamps her mouth shut.

"Tell me," I say, even though my heart is already hammering with fear. "Tell me what that means."

She sighs. "You were a last-ditch effort to work with the Nightmare," she says. "And I would argue—*did* argue—that you were a success. You got through to him, formed a connection. You didn't succumb to the nightmares. But the director disagrees. He thinks you proved that it is too dangerous to let anyone interact with him. He thinks the time has come to learn more through…other methods."

"Other methods," I repeat hollowly.

"Dissection," she says, not meeting my eyes. "And then autopsy."

Chapter Twenty-Six

I shut my eyes against a flood of sudden tears, sucking in a breath. "He can't," I whisper. "The Nightmare is…he's alive. He's intelligent. He's sentient, and—he's *kind*. The director can't treat him like this!"

"He knows," she says, her voice gentle. "Everyone up top knows, and they have known for a very long time. Most of the subjects are the same as your X-13, Mara. They think, they feel. They are not mindless beasts, and everyone knows it." She sighs, shutting her eyes for a moment before opening them again. Part of me wants to scream at her for allowing this to happen, but I can see the genuine pain in her expression. I remember the way she tried to guide me away from revealing what I knew to Director Ramsey, and I think I finally understand. She was trying to protect me…and show me how to fight from the inside, as she herself must be doing.

"The Director is aware, like all those who came before him. Like that asshole he hand-picked to succeed him." She must mean Ethan; the thought of him taking over this place makes me absolutely sick. "He has access to decades of files that prove it. Decades of people like you—like *me*—who realized that they're more than monsters. But it won't stop him. He sees them only as a means to an end. Something to be experimented with, and picked apart, until he can understand it well enough to use it."

"But why?" I ask, my voice trembling, barely a whisper. This truth is even more horrible than I could've imagined. "What is the meaning of this place, all of this research? What can it achieve other than cruelty?"

She shrugs, the gesture small and helpless, uncharacteristic of her. She looks as sad as I feel, like some wall within her is crumbling. "I wish I knew," she said. "I've been working here for a long time, Mara. But the more I learn, the harder I find it to understand. The best guess I have is that men like him hate anything that they can't control, whether it's monsters or women like us."

I think back to my encounters with the director, and I know she has a point. The things he did were cruel, yes—but even worse than that, there was a sadistic sort of glee in him. Like he found joy in toying with my emotions, putting me in my place. "He's a fucking sicko," I whisper. "How can you stand to work for him?"

"Because I have a plan," she says, her mouth firming with resolve as she looks at me. "A plan to bring in more people like you, then eventually destroy this place from the inside and rebuild it new, and better." Then the expression cracks a bit. "Well... I *had* a plan, that is. I'm afraid you've thrown a rather heavy wrench into it." She grimaces. "And I suspect the director knew all along. He ordered me to stay here, deactivated my security card..." She tosses aside the useless piece of plastic and glares at it. "I believe he intended for us both to die here."

Fear ripples through my chest. Is it possible he knew about

my plan, as well? I thought I was pulling this off, but maybe I was just being lured deeper into a trap. Still, there's nowhere to go but forward. "Well, *I'm* not ready to give up," I say.

For a moment she hesitates. Then she straightens, and I feel like she's figuratively brushing herself off and readying herself for another go. "No. Neither am I." She sighs, shuts her eyes before she speaks. "I wish you had come to me," she says. "I have a plan a long time in the making. I've worked so hard, gaining trust and power here, bringing in new hires like you and Belle in the hope you would someday be allies…"

"I *tried*, Calliope," I argue, thinking back to when I visited her house. "You lied to me."

She sighs, nods slightly. "I know. You're right. I thought it was too early to play my hand, but…look where that's led us." She folds her arms over her chest, forehead wrinkling in thought. "Well. The best-laid plans, as they say. But perhaps I can still salvage the pieces." She opens her eyes and her expression changes, like she's steeling herself. She lifts herself up from the chair and brushes herself off. She looks around, and I can sense the gears in her head turning. "Yes. Maybe this chaos will be good for something, after all." Her gaze settles on me again, and she takes a deep breath. "But we're going to need help." She turns to the control panel and presses a button to unlock a cell.

* * *

"I need to turn the temperature down first," Dr. Wright says, her hands darting over the control panel in the observation room for the cell she opened: X-11, the plaque reads. Through the viewing panel, I see an all-white room like the one that held the Nightmare, but bare except for a single metal chamber in the center. It looks like a huge chest freezer. "They have him in hibernation."

Though Dr. Wright's expression is as carefully controlled as always, her hands are trembling, and she keeps fixing her outfit like an anxious tic. Once she's done with the controls, she steps back and rests her hands on her hips, one foot tapping nervously against the tile.

"Is everything okay?" I ask.

She swallows. "Yes." At first I think she's going to leave it at that, but then she continues, "It's been a very long time since I was able to see him."

Realization hits me later than it should've. "This is the subject you had that 'close encounter' with."

She nods. "X-11," she says quietly. "X. The Alien." That sends a shock through me, but she continues without a pause. "And I...may not have been entirely honest with you," she confesses. But even if she hadn't, I could see it in the way her eyes hover on the viewing panel in front of her, the change in her normally icy demeanor.

"You care about him," I say softly.

"I always have." She bites her lip. "It's why I stayed working at this godforsaken facility. Why I tried so hard to claw my way up through the ranks. I knew I had to find a way to set him free. All these years, I've planned for it..." She glances at me, and her lips twist wryly. "And then came you."

I flush. "If you had told me..."

"I know. I should've told you the truth as soon as you opened up to me about your own feelings. I shouldn't have thrown you under the bus with Ramsey out of fear it would ruin my own plans. We could have worked together and prevented this. It's my own fault." She shakes her head. "Regardless, we're in this together now."

Before I can respond, there's a beep of an alarm from the control panel. Within the cell, the top of the chest freezer slides to the side. I hold my breath, realizing I'm about to get my first glimpse of an extraterrestrial being. At my side, Dr. Wright is frozen just like I am, her eyes locked on the chamber. For a moment, nothing happens. Then, a pale tentacle lifts out of the chamber, pokes tentatively at the air, and crawls over the side. Another emerges from the other side, and a creature lifts itself out.

I would've thought that seeing the Nightmare and the Minotaur would prepare me for more things that defy belief, but this is a new shock. It's hard to make sense of what I'm seeing at first. The creature is huge, and somewhat humanoid in shape, though its knees bend the wrong way and its arms are proportionally longer than a human's. Then there are the eight tentacles coming out of its back, whipping around the room as if exploring it. Its eyes are large and inky black in a bluish-white complexion, and its mouth is huge and full of prominent, sharp teeth.

I'm terrified, even after my encounters with the Nightmare taught me not to judge a creature by its appearance. But Dr. Wright practically throws herself at the door.

"Let me speak to him first," she says quickly, and before I can say anything, she's heading into the hallway, and then into the cell, shutting herself in alone with it.

Him, I remind myself. Dr. Wright said *him*.

She approaches the subject slowly, speaking soft words that I can't hear from outside of the cell, but the tenderness and fragile hope is obvious on her face. I press a hand to my mouth as the alien stands perfectly still, regarding her with a tense posture. She said it had been a long time, and it sounded like the history between them was complicated… What if she's wrong about him? What if his feelings have soured after years of being trapped here with her on the outside?

As the alien's tentacles abruptly lunge for her, I gasp and reach for the door handle, but then they grip her and draw her in with utmost gentleness, and the two embrace. He leans down to press his forehead against hers, and she melts against him, looking smaller and more vulnerable than I ever could've imagined.

To be honest, I was still hesitant about trusting Dr. Wright after she lied to me before. Nothing could've convinced me like seeing her with her own beloved subject; nobody can fake that kind of tenderness. I turn away to give them some privacy, because it feels like I'm intruding. But even as I will myself to give them some time to themselves, I'm all too aware of the seconds ticking by with Somnus still in danger somewhere.

Just when I'm about to turn around and barge in on them, privacy be damned, I hear the door open and turn to face them. To my surprise, it isn't an alien that emerges, it's a human man I don't recognize in a lab coat. There's something not *quite* right about him when I look harder, similar to the Siren. His bones are protruding a bit too much, his teeth a bit too sharp, an odd blankness to his expression. Dr. Wright is clasping one of his hands.

"Shapeshifter?" I ask, looking up at him.

"Yes," the strange man—alien… subject?—answers. He fixes pale eyes on me and the hair on the back of my neck stands on end. He really is vaguely unsettling, but I try to fight off my body's natural reaction of fear and force a smile instead.

"X is very talented," Dr. Wright says, glancing up at him fondly.

There's *so* much I want to ask about him, his origins, and the obvious affection between them. But Somnus is still in danger, so instead, I look at the shapeshifting alien and say, "I hope you can fight too."

He grins. For a moment, his eyes glint in the light, and his canines look far longer and sharper than they have a right to be. "Oh, yes."

I match his grin. "Good. Let's go get the Nightmare."

Chapter Twenty-Seven

D r. Wright leads us deeper into the heart of the facility, her alien stalking at her side. They make an odd duo—her so slim and proper in her business attire, him so tall and moving with an odd off-kilter gait—but they walk with a shared determination and a predatory sort of grace. They fall into the same rhythmic step without seeming to notice, while I hurry along behind them, trying to keep up and desperately wishing Somnus were here.

The hallways grow narrower, the doors sparser; it feels like we're traveling into a maze. It's all a bit dizzying, and I'm glad to have Dr. Wright here with me instead of trying to find my way through alone. Subject X-11, or *X*, as Dr. Wright calls him, is a steadying presence as well; unnerving and uncanny to look at, yes, but if he's anything like Somnus, I know we're lucky to have him on our side.

Yet still, I can't fight the sensation that I am only going further and further into enemy territory. The sort of place that someone doesn't come out of alive.

I can't stop thinking about what Dr. Wright said, and Somnus somewhere in this building, helpless and hurting, at Director Ramsey's mercy. I need to save him, no matter how dangerous it is. I don't know what will happen to me if I continue to pursue this path—even if we escape, what future can Somnus and I really have after this plan has gone so horribly, bloodily wrong?—but I do know that I refuse to live the rest of my life without him.

The depth of my feelings for him frightens me. I don't know when I started thinking about him as a necessary part of my life. He's far more than a monster, or a test subject, or a deliciously dark dream. The way I care about him is something I haven't let myself feel in a very long time. But even though it scares me to feel like this, now that I have him, I will *not* let him go.

Eventually, Dr. Wright brings us to another door. It has a thumb-imprint lock, rather than a keycard.

"This leads to Ramsey's personal working space," she says. "I've never had the clearance to enter. But..." She looks up at her alien. "If you could, X? Director Ramsey."

"I remember him well," X says, and raises one hand. It shifts in front of my eyes, and he presses a thumb to the pad. The door clicks open.

"Wait," I say. "If he can just turn into Ramsey, then he can stop this—"

"No," Dr. Wright says before I can even finish. "I'm sorry, truly, but we can't risk that right now." She meets my eyes, her own gaze steady. "I'll explain everything later. Right now, focus on getting to X-13. Then we can handle the rest."

I bite my tongue and we enter another control room.

It's smaller than the last but has video feeds covering areas that the last one lacked. It's fully abandoned, like the other one. Yet somehow I doubt the director fled the building when the chaos started. If anything, it may have driven him to proceed with his plan to dispose of the Nightmare more immediately.

My chest goes tight at the thought, and I frantically search the screens for signs of Somnus's shadowy form.

I suck in a startled breath as I finally see him. The camera feed is like something straight out of a horror movie. Somnus is strapped to a table. He flickers around the edges and shudders in agitation, in a way that reminds me of how he responded to sound 3 when I first tested it. The director must be using that noise to keep him contained and weak; I can't imagine how he could be held down like that otherwise.

Director Ramsey is standing in the room, looking down at him with a terrifyingly cold expression. On the wall behind him, I catch a glint of metal, and realize with a lurch of my stomach that it's a set of tools. Scalpels and saws and other surgical instruments made of a multitude of materials. Dr. Wright was correct: he intends to try to dissect the Nightmare, after somehow making him physical enough to contain in one form. Judging by how weak Somnus appears, he won't be able to defend himself.

I press a hand to the screen, wishing I could reach out to him. "There," I tell Dr. Wright, my voice wavering. "How do we get to him?"

When she doesn't respond immediately, I tear my eyes away from the terrible sight and look at her. Her attention, and that of X, are focused on a different screen, one featuring a group of armored, armed forces moving carefully through the halls.

"Shit," I whisper.

"Looks like he called in reinforcements," Dr. Wright says. She chews her lip as she glances through the other screens and pauses on one featuring the gore-stained Siren, wandering through the halls. "She'll slow them down, but I doubt she can stop them."

"What can we do?" I ask. "Is there any way to lock down the facility from here, prevent them from following us?"

She shakes her head. "If they're here at all, they're on the director's orders, and he's granted them full clearance." She jerks her head at the feed of him standing over the Nightmare. "And I would guess he knows we're here, and knows exactly what we're trying to do. They'll be coming for us."

"I am not going back to that cell," X snarls. When I look at him, I have to suppress a shudder; he looks less human now, his bones standing out starkly like they're trying to press through his skin. His eyes flash metallic and pupilless under the lights. "I am a warrior. I would rather die a warrior's death."

"No one is dying today, X," Dr. Wright says, sounding impossibly calm given the situation. She looks at him, and, even more impossibly, smiles. "Well, not us, at least. But it is time to fight."

"What?" I look back and forth between them. "You can't possibly mean to take them on. I… I can't ask you to do that." I don't know how strong X is, but I do know that there are a *lot* of people with very large guns on that screen. "You should run while you can."

"This isn't for you, darling," Dr. Wright says crisply. She holds the alien's gaze until he nods, and then turns to look at me. "Our plan hinges on this too. If the director has been paying attention, then he already knows I freed X. There is no turning back." She reaches up and lets her hair down, shaking it out around her shoulders. "We will hold them off as long as we can. You'll have to deal with the director and free the Nightmare on your own."

How? I want to ask. But this is my fight, and my responsibility. I nod. "I will," I say. "And we'll come help you as soon as we can."

"We can handle ourselves. Focus on your own monster." She slips a hand into X's, and without a further word, they walk out the door.

I watch them, and part of me wants to beg Dr. Wright not to go. To stay and help me, lend me her cool self-assurance and clear head. But I know that's unreasonably selfish. This mess is because of me, and it's my turn to take control of the situation. So I take a deep breath, push open the door, and head deeper into the facility alone.

* * *

The rest of the building felt abandoned, but this area feels even emptier. The air is colder, the lights dimmer, the walls and floor dark gray instead of white. A swollen silence fills the space, like the moment before something terrible happens in a horror movie. Director Ramsey's personal working space... I shudder to imagine what happens here.

I expect to find a nasty surprise waiting around every corner, but just like the screens in the control room showed, these halls are empty. I walk through the silence until I hear something staticky and strange. I follow the sound, my dread growing as it becomes louder and louder, turning into a high-pitched screech, and find the door at the end. It waits open.

A trap if I've ever seen one, but I have no choice but to step inside.

The moment I'm through the door, my eyes catch on the tools hanging on the far wall, and I know this is the room where I saw the director and Somnus. The light is shockingly bright, enough to make my eyes water. Quickly, my gaze shifts to the table and Somnus, strapped on it. He's limp at this point, his body strangely still and solid, matte black like the first time I used Sound 3 on him.

I rush over and fumble for the leather straps holding his arms and legs. When I touch him, his skin is strangely cold and hard, stiff like a corpse. He doesn't respond to my presence. I wish I could shut off that awful noise, which must be hurting him, but I can't. "Please," I whisper. "Wake up. I'm here, I'm finally here. Just like I promised."

It's strange, to think that I've never touched the Nightmare in real life before. He smells the same way he does in my dreams, that familiar scent of smoke and spice. He finally stirs weakly as I release the binds and try to lift him up. His eyes twitch toward me, and wispy tendrils of shadow reach for me. But it's obvious he's in no state to fight.

"I've got you," I murmur to him. "Hang on just a little while longer."

As I help him sit up, the door slams shut behind me. I turn and find the director there, a gun in his hand and aimed at me. Somnus shudders at my side, trying to lurch forward, but only my arm around his waist prevents him from falling. That awful noise is still screaming, keeping him weak.

"You arrogant girl," Director Ramsey says, pure hatred in his eyes. "I almost thought you couldn't possibly be foolish enough to take the bait, but Ethan was right. You did." He shakes his head. "You really thought you could waltz in here and take my property?"

"He's not property," I say. "You're the arrogant one for ever thinking he could *belong* to you." I gesture to the facility around us. "And that goes for all of them. It was only a matter of time before this crashed down on your head."

He laughs, the sound cold and mirthless. "You really think you can bring down everything I've built? *You?* Some pathetic girl with a twisted crush on a creature that would kill you at the first opportunity?" His lips twist into a sneer. "You're lucky I caught you and stopped you from getting the whole damn town killed. That thing slaughtered people when it escaped in the eighties. You really want to unleash a creature like that on Ash Valley?"

I think of those photographs that Dr. Wright showed me—twisted bodies with missing eyes, their faces distorted by terror—but push the memory away and tighten my grip around Somnus's waist. "He was hurt and scared and desperate," I say. "I know it was wrong, and so does he. He won't do it again."

"You think you know so much," the director says. "But you're basing this off nothing. Worse than nothing. You're basing it off sick fucking *fantasies*. Off *dreams*." He shakes his head in disgust. "Even if I hadn't lured you here to get rid of you, that creature would've done my work for me eventually."

"Dreams," I whisper, "are more powerful than you think." I will not let this man make me doubt myself. I will not let anyone do that to me again. I know who I am, and I know what I stand for, and I know that what I feel for Somnus is real. I trust him. And more importantly, I trust myself. "You might be right. He might hurt me, someday. But love *always* gives someone the power to hurt you. It is *always* frightening. But that's what it's all about…finding someone you can trust to keep your heart safe."

He stares at me a few moments longer. Then he shakes his head and pulls the trigger. The gunshot is so loud, it drowns out the screeching over the speakers.

I don't have time to move. No time to think. I didn't believe he would actually shoot me, so there's nothing I can do except flinch, shut my eyes, and brace myself for the pain.

But it doesn't come. After a moment, I open my eyes again and see, to my shock, a giant hand of shadow raised in front of me like a shield, extending from the Nightmare leaning heavily against my side. His claws slowly open, and a crushed bullet clinks to the floor. Then his body sags, his energy exhausted, his form collapsing into a wisp of a shadow.

The director's eyes bulge. His fingers tighten around the trigger again, but this time I'm prepared. I rush at him with a shout of fury. There is no logic in it, no plan, just anger. Pure feral rage, powered by all of the times I've felt scared and helpless in the face of this man and others like him. I raise a hand and wisps of shadows, the remnants of Somnus, drift over my arm and the backs of my fingers and extend in dark claws above my nails. I—*we*—swipe at the director and claw bloody rivets into his face and chest.

Director Ramsey screams, stumbling backward, the gun dropping from his hand and clattering to the tile.

I keep advancing on him as he retreats. I *feel* the Nightmare looming behind me, see the sharp-toothed, snarling shadow we cast over the wounded director, and feel a wicked glee rising within me. It is like the Nightmare gives life to my anger, gives an outlet for all of the pent-up frustration. So many times, in my life, I've been made to feel small; now, with Somnus at my side, I feel *powerful*.

It is a beautiful, freeing sensation, to be one with Somnus. Neither of us would be strong enough to face him alone, but together? Together we are invincible.

"You stupid little bitch," the director spits even as he retreats from us. His back hits the wall, and he cowers as blood drips from his wound, but still there's pure fury in his eyes. It must grate, to be taken down by someone you feel nothing but contempt for.

I grin at him. As the Nightmare brushes a shadowy tendril against the back of my neck, I can almost hear his dark chuckle in my ear.

Then the director's attention shifts to the door. I follow a moment later—to see it opening again. A sound splits the air, a high ringing, much louder than the one already playing over the speakers. I wince, clapping a hand over my ear, more annoyed than anything…but the Nightmare *shrieks*, a horrible sound, and recoils into a thin haze around my neck, burrowing against me as if trying to hide.

I look up and see Ethan standing in the doorway, a radio gripped in his shaking hand. He steps toward us, kicking the door shut behind him.

"Ethan, *stop!*" I scream at him as the Nightmare shudders and twitches against the back of my neck. Not even my shout can drown the noise out now. It's so loud it hurts *my* ears, reverberates in my bones. Somnus slowly slips away from my neck, and when I try to catch him, he slides through my fingers like water to pool on the floor. He was barely strong enough to hold himself together with my help before. Now, with this double assault on his senses, he is hardly a wisp of smoke and still fading in front of my eyes. He retracts into a tiny ball of shadow and begins to turn hard and brittle again. Solid, unable to shift—*vulnerable*. This must be what the director wanted, a way to keep him solid and dissect him.

"Mara, sweetie." Ethan has to raise his voice to be heard

above that god-awful screeching from the radio, yet still he manages that voice of dripping condescension. "You don't know what you're doing. I'm sorry I helped set you up, but trust me, it's for your own good."

I grit my teeth. I hate that even now, those words in that tone wring an automatic reaction out of me: tears pricking the backs of my eyes, doubt curdling in my heart. *I'm just trying to protect you, Mara. I know what's best for you, Mara. Oh, Mara, you can't do anything on your own, can you?*

All of these fucking men. They love to treat me like I don't know any better. Like I'm just some poor, misguided little girl who can't *possibly* know something that they don't. Surely I need a firm hand and a superior hand to guide me. If they hurt me, it's only for my own good.

After his condescending dismissal, Ethan doesn't spare me a glance. All of his attention is focused on the Nightmare shuddering in pain on the floor. Like I'm not a threat.

Which means he doesn't notice as I bend down and pick up the director's fallen gun. Or even when I aim in his direction.

"Ethan," I say. "Shut the radio off. Now."

Then, finally, he looks at me. His eyes widen, but his expression is more incredulous than scared.

"What do you think you're going to do with that?" he asks, in the tone of someone speaking to a child. "Put it down before someone gets hurt."

"Shut. Off. The sound," I grit out, the gun steady in my hands even as my pulse pounds in my ears.

I've only shot a gun a few times before, and certainly not at another person, or under such stress. But honestly? It'd be hard to miss at this range. I just hope Ethan doesn't force me to kill him. He may be a huge fucking asshole, but that doesn't mean I want a dead body on my conscience.

"You don't understand the situation," he says slowly, taking a small step toward me and away from the Nightmare. With the radio angled away, the Nightmare seems to recover slightly. Good. But the director is pulling himself together, too, reaching into his pocket, likely for another weapon.

"I understand much more than you do," I snarl at Ethan. "I don't have time for this. Last warning. *Shut it off.*"

"You know I can't—"

I fire before he finishes the sentence. For a moment, there's only a dull ringing in my ears, muffling any other sounds, while Ethan stares at me in shock. I stare back, surprised myself, even though I knew exactly what I was doing when I pulled that trigger.

Then both of our gazes shift to the bloody ruin of his hand. The radio clatters to the tile, and Ethan lets out a strangled groan and clutches his mangled fingers to his chest with an expression of disbelief. I dart forward and stomp on the radio—once, twice, until the metal crunches and the sound dies off with a last crackle of static. When I turn around, breathing hard, I realize I'm only a few steps away from Ethan. His face is drained of color and twisted in fury.

"You bitch," he says, tottering forward a step. "You stupid goddamn whore. I'm going to—"

Then his eyes roll back, and he faints. I take a step back and watch as he collapses to the floor in a heap, his head thumping against the tile and his limp, wounded hand flopping to one side.

"Huh," I mutter, shrugging, and then step over him and to the side of the Nightmare. He is still in the form of an orb, shivering as he recovers. I reach down, extending a hand. The orb melts into long, clawed fingers, which reach up to tangle with mine. Shadows wind slowly around my hand and up my arm with the sinuous movements of a snake. "You're all right now," I murmur. "No one's going to hurt you."

I turn to the director, who is pressed back against the wall and staring at me with bulging eyes.

"You," he rasps, glancing from Ethan's fallen form to my face. "You are…utterly insane. You deserve to be locked up like these fucking monsters. And when all of this is over—when we catch you—you will be." His expression darkens, his eyebrows drawing together and his lip curling. "I will make sure of it personally. No matter where you run, I will find you."

I look down at the gun still in my hand but then toss it aside. Instead, I idly stroke the Nightmare's skin, which is turning warm and velvety. A hand reaches out of the shadows pooling on my arm, and then a body, and a face, his expression icy and determined as he peels off my side in his own humanoid form. I smile at him and then look over and meet the director's eyes.

"You're the one who's going to be running," I say. I slowly walk over to him, enjoying the feeling of standing over him. Somnus hovers at my back, his eyes on me. He could be tearing the director apart right now, but instead he waits to see what I say. Part of me, admittedly, wants to watch Somnus tear this man apart. But maybe it would be just as good to prove to him that Somnus isn't, and never was, the monster he thought. "We're going to give you one chance—"

With a shout, the director pulls a scalpel out of his pocket and lunges at me on his hands and knees. I throw out a hand, stumbling back, and the blade slashes a shallow cut across my palm. Somnus lunges forward, snapping his teeth, and the director scuttles back against the wall again.

I stare down at the blood dripping from my hand and then look at Somnus. He stands poised over the director, huge hands braced on the wall, his teeth bared. Still, he waits. I know, in this moment, that what I've argued so many times is true: the Nightmare is not some monstrous killer by nature. Even with this man, who hurt him so badly and tried to kill me, he is holding back.

But in this case, to be honest, I'm not so sure he should.

"Well," I say. "That was your one chance." I clench my hand despite the throb of pain. "Go on, Somnus."

Director Ramsey opens his mouth to say something. But before he can get a word out, the Nightmare opens his jaws. Stretching his mouth inhumanly wide, like a snake, he bites his head right off.

Chapter Twenty-Eight

The Nightmare and I curl up, exhausted, on the floor. The room is drenched in gore, and the stench grows by the minute; Ethan's unconscious body is still sprawled near us, along with the director's headless corpse. It's all a bit gross, but I am too tired and too relieved to move. Somnus's darkness both cradles me and drapes over me, like a warm blanket of shadow. I half doze against his broad chest while his claws stroke my hair. The more time we spend recovering like this, the stronger he becomes.

Too tired to speak, I gaze up at him and raise my uninjured hand in a simple sign: *I love you.*

He raises his large, clawed hand and mirrors the gesture. Then his palm closes over my fingers and he draws my hand to press against his heart.

I'm not sure how much time passes until we hear the door open. I jolt upright and then scramble to my feet, heart racing. It's hard to feel afraid with the Nightmare looming behind me, his hands gripping my shoulders to reassure me that he's here.

As soon as I hear the telltale click of heels, I relax, and gesture to the Nightmare to stand down. I can sense his puzzlement, but he listens anyway, draping over my shoulders and nuzzling against my neck.

Dr. Wright enters the room first, wearing her reclaimed heels and looking far more composed than anyone should be in this situation. She stops short as she enters the room, eyes flicking from me and the Nightmare at my back, to the headless body of Director Ramsey on the floor, to Ethan's unconscious form slumped nearby.

Her alien companion is close behind. X is covered head to toe with blood, with the gore especially concentrated around his mouth. Dr. Wright is splattered with it as well, though less than I'd expect. Thankfully, neither of them appear hurt.

X moves between her and us when he spots us, but Dr. Wright's expression is relieved.

"You actually did it," she marvels, and shows a rare, thin-lipped smile.

The alien, however, bares his teeth in our direction, letting out an inhuman rattling sound from somewhere deep in his throat. Dr. Wright reaches out a hand to soothe him, but the Nightmare is already rearing up at my back in response. The room darkens as he spreads out and responds with his own low growl.

"Hey, now," I say, reaching behind me. Shadowy fingers twine with mine, and I squeeze reassuringly. "It's all right. We're all on the same side."

The alien speaks in a language made up of mostly strange clicks and thrums I couldn't possibly replicate, and then spits out in English, "Foul creature. Demon."

"X." Dr. Wright puts a hand on his shoulder, and though he doesn't relax, his eyes do slide away from the Nightmare to meet hers. She gives him a pointed look. "I assure you that X-13 is neither a demon nor any threat to us, and that is quite enough posturing."

X slowly closes his lips back over his teeth and turns away, sulky. Somnus relaxes as well, though he stands closer than before, clearly on edge.

Dr. Wright and I exchange an exasperated look. *Men*, I'm sure she's thinking, just as I am.

"We don't have much time until the new wave of security forces arrives," Dr. Wright says, nodding her chin at the director's body. "Let's proceed with the plan, X. It's messy, but it'll still work."

He nods and steps forward to kneel next to the body.

"Please look away," he says in his curiously toneless voice.

"What are you going to do?" I ask. I can't help myself, even though I'm pretty sure I don't want to know.

"I must consume him," he says. "Do not worry. I do not make a habit of eating humans. I find it unsavory to eat intelligent creatures. However, this is necessary."

Dr. Wright takes my hand and turns me gently away. "Trust us," she says.

I swallow back nausea, nod, and shut my eyes. A moment later, I wish I had covered my ears, too, since the wet crunching that follows is probably going to haunt me forever. But a couple of minutes later, it's over. When I turn around with Dr. Wright again, all that remains of the director is a scalpel sitting on a bloodstained floor. The Alien straightens up, and his form shifts again, bones shifting and skin rippling as he changes into the spitting image of the director.

I gasp with the realization. "This was your plan. He's going to replace Director Ramsey, permanently."

Dr. Wright smiles, looking immensely satisfied. "Yes. This is why we couldn't proceed until Ramsey was gone. Having two of them would have been suspicious." She steps forward and touches the Alien's new face. He leans into her touch in a distinctly un-director-like way. *At least he's objectively handsome,* I think queasily, though I'm not sure I'll ever be able to shed my association with the real man.

"I admire your dedication to setting your Nightmare free," Dr. Wright continues after a moment, looking at me. "But as I mentioned before, it is not as simple as that. Most of the subjects here are not ready for the outside world, and the world is certainly not ready for them. Some, like my X, and your Nightmare, have experience with humans, and the skill sets to blend in or hide themselves from the public. But others, like the Siren you met, are not so lucky. And they are no less deserving of freedom from the director's barbaric methods. I could not bear the thought of leaving them to suffer at his hands." She looks down at Ethan and wrinkles her nose. "And that protégé of his, I'm sure, would be no better. But setting them free would lead to disaster."

"So instead, you decided to take over the whole operation," I breathe. She must have put so much time and thought into planning this, patiently awaiting an opportunity…and then I came along and blew it all up.

"Precisely," she says, and smiles at me. "Together, X and I will change things around here. Run it our way. We will seek to rehabilitate the subjects rather than torture them in the name of science. I believe many of these so-called monsters are like X or the Nightmare. They can think, and learn, and feel, and eventually live alongside humans peacefully. But first, they need to meet the right person to teach them that humanity is not merely something to fear, or to prey upon, as the case may be." Her smile has a sly edge. "If ours are any indication, it seems that the gentle touch of a woman, rather than a man with a scalpel, may be enough to do the trick."

I blush. I always had an inkling that she knew more about the nature of my relationship with Somnus than she let on, and this just about confirms it. Then again, judging from what I've witnessed between her and the alien she calls "X," it's only because she's a kindred spirit with her own…experiences, shall we say.

"And what does that mean for us?" I ask. I reach back for the Nightmare, and he squeezes my hand. When I glance sideways, he's fully formed his humanoid body again and is waiting at my side, his eyes on Dr. Wright.

"That depends on what you want," she says. "I plan on framing today's events as a security breach. I will say that the Siren, Minotaur, and Alien were able to escape their cells. That the first was recaptured, the second killed in self-defense, and the latter disappeared into the night. Given his shapeshifting nature, it will likely be impossible to track him down." She studies the Nightmare. "I could say the same about your subject if you like. Of course, there will be intense scrutiny and suspicion placed on you. I cannot save you from that if I wish to hide my own involvement. You will have to hide the Nightmare carefully. You may wish to flee the country."

There's a lump in my throat at the thought. I was prepared to do what I had to do, for the sake of freeing the Nightmare…but she's right, I doubt I could stay here in Ash Valley with Somnus at my side. Someone would catch onto us eventually. And now that the time has come, I find myself reluctant to abandon my hometown. For all that I've complained about it, I've come to know a new side of the town since I moved back here. My parents, my friends, my work here… I'd have to abandon it all if I were to flee. "Or?" I prompt, because it seems like more coming.

She smiles. "Or you could stay here. Assist us in changing this place, and helping to rehabilitate the subjects who reside here." She glances at Somnus and inclines her head slightly. "Both of you, I suspect, would be useful in this endeavor. And both of you, of course, would be treated as valuable employees, not test subjects. Never again."

Chapter Twenty-Nine

I stumble down an endless, twisting hallway, with a Nightmare close behind. No matter how fast I run, or how many corners I turn, he is always just behind me. Closer and closer with every thump of my heart, his claws extending toward me.

Finally, he catches me, one huge hand wrapping around my waist and lifting me off the floor. I only have time for one desperate cry of surprise before he shoves me to the ground. He rips my panties off with one claw and holds me down as he pushes into me from behind. I cry out with mingled pain and pleasure that soon turn entirely to the latter.

* * *

Afterward, he carries me back to bed. I nuzzle into his velvety-soft chest, sore and exhausted and thoroughly sated. "My Nightmare," I murmur.

He grips me tighter. "My dreamer." He keeps me in his arms as he settles onto the bed, and we both curl up together. His shadowy tendrils flicker over my body, soothing the spots that ache.

"It's almost morning," he says.

"What?" It feels impossible, but when I peel my eyes open and look at the window, he's right. "Ugh," I grumble. "Can't we stay here forever?"

I feel him smile against the back of my neck. "Wake, my love. We have work to do."

I wake up alone, sunlight streaming through the window… and my panties lying in a shredded heap of fabric at the bottom of the bed.

I sigh. "These things are expensive, you know," I grumble to the empty room.

I stand and stretch, luxuriating in the feeling of freedom that comes with my new studio apartment. My mattress rests on the floor, and most of my stuff is still in boxes. But the view of the desert landscape is gorgeous, I already put up a few horror movie posters, and it's starting to feel like home.

Smiling, I head to the shower to get ready for the day.

* * *

I walk into the Facility on time. Unlike past mornings, the atmosphere in the front lobby is relaxed, and a few of my coworkers are hanging around and chatting amiably. No more secrecy, no more isolation.

"Good morning, Mara," Ezra calls, as bright-eyed as usual. He peels away from the rest of the group and deposits a brown butter maple latte from Cup o' Happy into my hand.

"You're a lifesaver," I groan, and take a nice long sip that scalds my tongue and fills my belly with warmth and sweetness.

His morning coffee runs are a small but certainly enjoyable perk of the *new* way things work around here.

"Late night?" he asks, and winks.

I grin back, mime zipping my lips, and approach the others waiting.

Dr. Wright is in the midst of an argument with Belle. She and Ezra were among the few employees that our new director didn't purge from the facility, on my recommendation.

"It's eaten all of its other handlers," Dr. Wright is saying.

"*She*," Belle retorts, eyes flashing with an energy I rarely see from her, "has eaten all of the *men* she's been forced to work with, yes. But I'll be different."

I slip past them so I won't disturb their conversation but give Belle a thumbs-up behind Dr. Wright's back. She smiles at me, tucking a strand of hair behind her ear, and then returns to making her case. I suspect she's going to win in the end.

I carry on past security, which currently sits empty. We had to fire most of the guards, along with the vast majority of the researchers, ostensibly for the disaster of the Minotaur's escape and murder spree.

I am concerned that one of them may come back to bite us later, but there's no better way. We can't know who might notice that the director is acting differently; X-11 is good, but he's not perfect, and his speech especially is noticeably different. Plus, most of them are too used to the way this place *used* to be, with all of its restrictions and cruelties. Dr. Wright has been slowly filling the empty roles with new faces. She's been talking about figuring out ways to do more local outreach for security work, too, and maybe sponsoring some young Ash Valleyans' college degrees in return for a contract to work here for a few years. It's clear she really has been thinking of this for a long, long time—she has a lot of great ideas, and so far everything is being implemented quickly and efficiently.

Ethan, of course, was fired along with the rest. I wasn't there to witness the firing itself, but I did see him walking out that day, with his hand bandaged. The moment he saw me, he went pale and hurried away, which felt pretty good. I'm still a little worried that I haven't seen the last of him yet, but at least he has a strict NDA restraining him from retaliating publicly.

I'm excited to watch this place transform and, hopefully, blossom. If things go well, it will be good for everyone: the employees, the locals, and most of all, the subjects.

Speaking of which… There is one more perk I'm particularly pleased about.

I head to my office to set down my coffee and then knock at the adjoining door. It slides open a moment later, revealing a dark, windowless room.

I step inside without fear, letting my eyes adjust to the lack of light until I find the spot of darkness that's more solid than the rest. A shadowy figure coalesces in the center of the room.

Good morning, Mara, he signs.

"Good morning, Somnus," I say, and smile. "Ready to get to work?"

I reach out and take his clawed hand in mine.

Acknowledgments

This is my first foray into the world of self-publishing, and this book never would have been possible without a lot of support along the way.

I would like to thank:

My developmental editor Sarah Chorn, who is incredibly insightful and a delight to work with.

My eagle-eyed copyeditor Claudette Cruz ("The Editing Sweetheart"), for her attention to detail and patience with me.

My early beta readers Angela Deaton, jenna_hackett, and Top-Turnip-4057, who took a chance on a random Reddit post and were immensely helpful in taking this story from an early draft to a polished story.

The immensely talented Impyeu for this *amazing* cover. You brought my babies to life!! (Check her out on Instagram, @1mpyeu!)

The Podium team and narrator Rachel Leblang, for the excellent audiobook edition of the story.

The Romance Author's Writing Group Discord, a community that was endlessly kind, welcoming, and eager to help along my journey.

My supportive parents, including my dad (who I hope never reads this, oh god) and my mom (who, when asked if she wanted a censored version, said "I'm in my fifties, I think I can handle it").

My partner, my favorite person in the world, for always being at my side and supporting me through several small meltdowns over the course of writing this book. I love you!

And last but not least: everyone who has read this far. Thank you, dear reader, for choosing my weird little love story. I hope you enjoyed it.

About the Author

Skyla Gray is a romance author fond of all things scary and steamy. When not writing, she can usually be found gaming, cooking, or binge-watching horror movies. She lives in Arizona with her partner and an absolute rascal of a dog.

Sign up for my newsletter for an extra spicy bonus scene featuring Mara and Somnus after the events of The Nightmare's Kiss!

You can connect with me on:

🌐 http://skyla-gray.com

Subscribe to my newsletter:

✉ https://skyla-gray.ck.page/e838b44108

Also by Skyla Gray

Want more of the Monster Research Facility? Meet a new researcher x monster couple in...

Book 2: The Revenant's Heart
Can a dead heart learn to beat again?

After dropping out of med school, Lucy Sullivan thought her skill with a scalpel would only be useful for her hobbyist taxidermy. But life takes another unexpected turn when she becomes the doctor for a most unusual patient: one who's already dead. Or undead, rather.

Subject X-14, "The Revenant" - aka Victor - may be a collection of stitched-together corpses with a hunger for human flesh, yet Lucy soon finds herself grappling with unexpected fondness for her patient. In spite of her general fear of getting close to people, she wants to make him happy just as badly as she wants to cut him open and figure out what makes him tick.

But when Victor uses her as a hostage and kidnaps her, Lucy becomes a pawn in his plot to take out his cruel creator. They say if you seek revenge, you should dig two graves - and with Lucy caught up in this scheme, it might just be three. Can she save Victor before he loses himself to his desire for vengeance, or will he drag her down with him?